STORIES FROM FIREFLY ISLAND

Also by Benedict Blathwayt

Bruno's Band
Bear's Adventure
Bear in the Air
Tangle and the Firesticks
Tangle and the Silver Bird
The Little House by the Sea

STORIES FROM FIREFLY ISLAND

Benedict Blathwayt

Julia MacRae Books

LONDON SYDNEY AUCKLAND JOHANNESBURG

for CHARLES, JOAN and HELEN

First published in Great Britain 1992
by Julia MacRae
an imprint of the Random Century Group
20 Vauxhall Bridge Road, London, SW1V 2SA

Random Century Australia (Pty) Ltd
20 Alfred Street, Milsons Point, Sydney, NSW 2061

Random Century New Zealand Ltd
PO Box 40–086, Glenfield, Auckland 10,
New Zealand

Random Century South Africa (Pty) Ltd
PO Box 337, Bergvlei 2012, South Africa

Typeset by 🅰 Tek Art Ltd
Addiscombe, Croydon, Surrey

Printed and bound in Great Britain by
Butler & Tanner Ltd, Frome and London

British Library Cataloguing in Publication Data
Blathwayt, Benedict
I. Title
Stories from Firefly Island
823.914[J]

ISBN 1–85681–012–7

Contents

I
FIREFLY ISLAND

O n warm nights the animals of Firefly Island would gather on the beach at the edge of the forest and ask Tortoise for a story. Tortoise had many memories and many stories.

"Tell us why the frogs croak at night," they would say. "Tell us the story of Lizard's race and of the great storm; about Big Bottlenose and Brave Pig."

Tortoise was wise, Tortoise knew almost everything. "What is the moon?" the animals sometimes asked. "What are the stars? Tell us why we are here, and where we come from."

Tortoise would blink and take a while to answer. He was old, very old, but not old enough to know that their island had once been molten rock and bare of any life at all, that the sea had risen and fallen many times, that the land had joined and unjoined. Tortoise had not been here to see the first seeds and nuts arrive, blown on the wind or carried by tides. Grasses, bushes and trees had sprouted from sand-filled cracks in the rock, and eventually insects and birds came to their branches.

Tortoise could tell them only that their ancestors had always been here; that the island was all there was upon the sea; that the sea itself stretched flat, the same for ever and ever, and the sky, too, spread outwards endless and empty.

Tortoise supposed the moon was a cluster of glow-worms and each star a bright firefly asleep on the blackness of the night: surely this was how it was – and it would always be the same.

The animals loved Tortoise. "Tell us another story," they said.

"About us!" giggled the monkeys. "Tell a story about us."

Tortoise frowned, the other animals sighed, for monkeys meant trouble. But Tortoise told them a story . . .

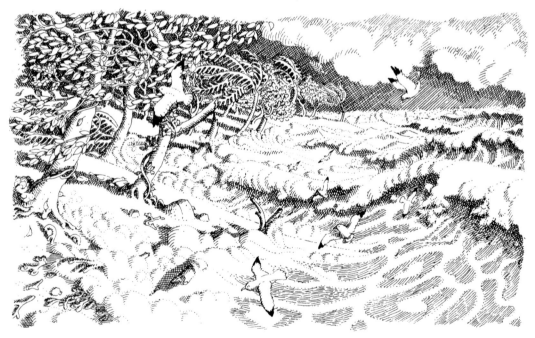

Many years ago there was a terrible storm, a storm that rocked every branch of every tree and sent waves foaming into the fringe of the forest itself.

With the whistle of the wind howling right through the night, and the rain lashing every hole and crevice, none of the island's animals got any sleep at all.

By morning they were exhausted. The storm died away, the sea grew calm, the sun came out and the whole forest steamed. Every bird and creature dried itself and then fell thankfully asleep, a long deep sleep that lasted until sunset.

Now, while most of the animals were still tired enough at the end of that day of recovery to settle down as usual for a good night's rest – the monkeys were NOT. They felt completely refreshed. They swung through the branches and hooted and howled and chattered and joked. What a noise! They carried on like this until dawn, so that nobody else on the whole island got any rest at all. And the following day, of course, they fell asleep in the hot sun, while the other animals had to busy themselves in their daily search for food.

And when did those monkeys wake up again? Just as the sun went down.

It became a dreadful habit: they slept by day and played by night. The storm had upset the rhythm of the island. The monkeys just laughed when the others begged them to be quiet.

It was all very well for the monkeys: they managed to grab fruit as they swung through the trees; even with a thin moon they could see well enough. *They* didn't go hungry. But the birds couldn't fly at night and it was too dark for some of the animals, too cold for others. Day was the time to feed, night was the time to sleep – it had always been that way.

"What are we going to do?" the animals asked each other in desperation. They settled down to think of a plan.

The finches suddenly had an idea. They told Grass-snake and Lizard. The chipmunks and porcupines agreed; so did the deer and the wild pigs. Everyone thought it a very good plan, everyone except the frogs who no-one had bothered to tell. The frogs seemed to get left out of everything – perhaps because they lived in far-off wet and boggy places where nobody else wanted to go.

Wild Pig asked the finches: "When are we going to have this concert?"

"Tomorrow," said the finches, "at sunrise."

The next morning, full of fruit and tired out from their night of fooling about, the monkeys settled down to sleep. The sun was warm, how peaceful they felt.

Then the finches gave the signal to begin. Already gathered beneath the trees where the monkeys slept, every creature on the island began to sing. If they couldn't sing, then they began to squeak, to snort, to bellow, or to grunt. The leaves of the trees shook with the noise of it all. The monkeys woke and held on tightly to their branches. At first they didn't know what was happening. The singing echoed from cliff top to tree top and back again.

"Quiet please!" shrieked the monkeys. "We're tired, we want to sleep!"

But the animals' concert went on. It was no use the monkeys blocking their ears or moving to a further tree; the orchestra of animals followed below them.

"Please let us rest," begged the monkeys, "it's been a long night, we need our sleep." But the chorus of voices kept singing and the pelicans brought fruit and water for dry throats.

"How long is this going to go on?" groaned the monkeys. All day, thought the finches to themselves, but they said nothing.

And that's just how long the concert lasted – all day. Towards sunset the noise grew wilder, more ragged and disorganised. But no quieter. The monkeys were desperate from lack of sleep. "We shall go mad!" they whimpered.

As the sun dipped into the sea, bit by bit the singing faded. The exhausted animals shut their eyes and fell asleep. And as the last voice died away, the monkeys too were finally able to sleep.

Such a hush and stillness fell over the island that you might have wondered if anything lived there at all. But there was still one remaining noise – a bubbly, piping sound from the island's damp places. It was the frogs. No one had told them about the concert, they had been asleep all day, too deep in the mud to have heard anything, and they were now just waking up.

But it was not an unpleasant noise and the other animals were too tired to be annoyed. One thing was certain: they could not spend another whole day singing, just so the frogs would sleep at night. Once was quite enough.

All the animals, including the monkeys, slept right through the night. And when the sun rose, they all awoke. Except the frogs of course, they were just falling asleep!

And that's the way it has been ever since.

II
BRAVE PIG

Wild Pig blushed – somebody had asked Tortoise for the story of Brave Pig.

"Do you mind if I tell it?" asked Tortoise kindly.

Pig shrugged, he didn't really mind; after all, it had happened a long time ago.

So Tortoise told the story . . .

Once, long ago, Wild Pig had been a bully. He was a mean, spiteful, self-satisfied show-off. He thundered through the ferns and grasses of the island's forest frightening the jungle-fowl and chipmunks out of their skins. He would only laugh at the flurry of feathers and their terrified squeaks. Pig, after all, was afraid of nothing.

The lizards and squirrels, deer and porcupine, all disliked this particular wild pig. They could never curl up safely in a patch of sunlight on the mossy forest floor, for it was quite likely that Pig, with a snort and delighted squeal, would come galloping through the undergrowth and leap right over them – or, more often, leap not quite far enough and land right on top of them. Pig's hooves were hard and his tusks very sharp.

He never seemed able to apologise for his clumsiness. By night or day, scaring the island animals out of their wits seemed to him to be one huge joke. According to Pig, no-one was as fearless and intelligent as himself; no-one could run round the island quicker; no-one was quite as sensible, agile or handsome as he.

Pig thought he was absolutely perfect.

One dark night, with a broad piggish grin on his snout, Pig woke up one of the shy deer as she slept peacefully in a clearing. He chased her in and out the tree trunks, slashing at the ivy and creeper with his tusks, this way and that, squealing as only a wild pig can.

"Afraid, eh?" he cried with a laugh. "Coward! Coward!"

To the deer he seemed like a bad dream come to life. Quail and Pheasant comforted the little deer when at last she stopped running in circles. Her black nose twitched and her dainty legs quivered in fear.

"If only there was a way we could show Pig up, in front of all the other animals on the island," said Quail, "if we could just make him see what it's like to be made a fool of."

"What we need to do is to frighten Pig," said Pheasant.

So, bobbing and pecking on the forest floor, they hatched a plan.

Quail did not roost at sunset that evening. When it was dark she went to a clearing in the forest where she knew the glow-worms gathered.

"I badly need your help," she said to them, as the little beetles moved among the leaves, their tails glowing bright green, "we are all being terrorised by Wild Pig."

But the glow-worms didn't seem very interested in her plan. Quail became quite severe. "Normally," she said, "we jungle fowl are asleep by now, so we don't have the opportunity to eat you glow-worms. But, if that were somehow to change . . . and staying up late became an unfortunate habit . . ."

"We'll help," said the glow-worms, quickly. "We're ready when you give the call."

Pheasant, meanwhile, had been to see one of the monkeys; they were known to be clever with their hands. Monkey thought Pheasant's plan a good joke and he also agreed to help.

Finally, Quail talked with the young deer who had been badly treated by Pig and asked her if she was brave enough to lure Pig down to the big rock by the drinking pool.

"Flatter him," said Quail. "Say how brave and strong he is; ask him to escort you to the pool because you are thirsty – yet afraid of the dark and of monsters and dream-beasts that may lurk in the shadows. He is so vain he will be unable to refuse you."

The young deer said yes, she too would help in curing Pig of his nastiness.

The next afternoon, on the slope of the big rock by the drinking pool, Monkey painted an enormous face; a face with jagged teeth and horrible eyes. No-one could see the face because Monkey had drawn it with a pointed stick dipped in wild honey, but the glow-worms would easily be able to find the sweet sticky lines of the drawing.

Now every part of Quail's plan was ready.

That night there was no moon. It was very dark. "Good luck everyone," clucked Quail.

The young deer looked for Pig. He was easy to find, snorting and grunting as he nosed the ground in search of tender roots.

"What do *you* want?" he asked gruffly when he saw the deer.

"Oh, brave handsome Pig," said Deer meekly, "I need your help. It's a hot night and I'm thirsty, but it's so dark that I'm quite lost and unable to find my way to the drinking pool."

"Well, you'll have to stay thirsty," said Pig rudely, "I'm busy."

"I only asked," Deer went on, "because your courage is well known to all of us. You are strong and wise and scared of nothing."

"That may well be true," said Pig, looking up for a moment, "but a pig has to eat. I told you, I'm busy. Go away."

"You see," said Deer, not giving up yet, "I have asked everyone else to lead me to the pool and no-one will help. The forest is too dark tonight and they are afraid of what terrible unknown things might lie in wait."

"A lot of nonsense!" snuffled Pig.

"Oh, if only I was as brave as you!" sighed Deer.

"Just a hoof-load of old stories," said Pig, "invented in order to keep youngsters at home."

"Oh Pig," said Deer, "if only I could convince myself of that. Of course," she added, "the others did say that even you would refuse. On a night as black as this, they all said, even Pig will feel a little afraid and stay in his lair and tell you to leave him in peace until morning."

"Oh," snorted Pig, thoughtfully, "they said that?"

"Yes," sighed Deer, in mock despair, "and I suppose they were right; it was just too much to ask after all; one couldn't expect it, even of the bravest Pig."

Deer began to wander away into the shadows.

"Wait a moment," grunted Pig, "you are obviously such a nervous weakling that I've decided to change my mind. Follow me."

So Pig set off, his snout searching out the scented forest trails that led to the drinking pool. As Deer followed, she noticed Pig seemed slightly on edge. Sometimes he would stop and listen. "What's that?" he'd ask; the merest rustle of leaves or flutter of moths made him jump.

"Oh Pig," whispered Deer, "I am so afraid."

"No need," snuffled Pig, "no need." But he didn't sound very sure of himself.

"Are you certain that there are no such things as monsters of the night?" asked Deer, as she followed him.

"Of course," Pig replied, his tusks chattering a little, "of course I'm sure."

They came into the clearing by the drinking pool. All was quiet except for the gurgling of the spring at the foot of the smooth rock face; except for the 'cluck' from a quail roosting somewhere in the Rizzleberry tree. Pig himself felt rather uneasy; he was secretly glad that Deer was there with him.

That quiet call from Quail had been a signal to the waiting glow-worms: they had already taken up their positions on the lines of honey drawn by Monkey; the whole of the rock-face was thick with them. On hearing Quail's signal, all together they lit their tails.

There, out of the blackness, towering above Pig and Deer, a huge and hideous green face appeared!

Pig's scream echoed round and round the island. Everyone heard it. He was off, crashing blindly through the undergrowth, tripping and skidding, his little hooves carrying him away from the terrible glowing beast faster than he had ever been before.

Many of the animals who had hidden in the bushes around the drinking pool began cheering and laughing: what a sight it had been, Brave Pig in a panic! He would never live it down.

Tortoise had found Pig the next morning, cowering miserably in his lair. Although Pig knew it had all been a tease, his teeth still chattered. What disgrace he felt.

"Never mind," said Tortoise, "cheer up. I'm sure that if you can forgive us, then we can all forgive you."

Pig had looked up then, with a glimmer of hope in his moist eyes. "I am going to change," he said.

And he did.

Tortoise had come to the end of his story.

"You can all see," said Pig, rather embarrassed, "that although I'm still a bit clumsy, I am nevertheless a completely new and likeable animal – considerate, brave, modest; improving all the time."

Tortoise smiled. "Dear Pig," he said, "I don't know what we would do without you."

III
SNOW

Tortoise loved the moon, and he loved the sea. On moonlit nights the foam washing in on the edge of the waves seemed as white and rounded as snow.

On just such a night, when the animals had followed Tortoise down to the beach, one of the chipmunks was reminded of his favourite story: "Tell us about snow, Tortoise," he squeaked, "please tell us."

It had only snowed once on Firefly Island, as far as anyone could remember; as far as Tortoise could remember anyway – and wasn't he the oldest and wisest of them all?

So Tortoise settled down in the damp sand and told them the story of the snow.

In a burrow under the toadleaf tree there once lived a fat chipmunk. This chipmunk didn't join in the great games of chase and tag that were carried on by the squirrels in the lower branches of the trees. Nor did she seem to want to play hide-and-seek in and out the boulders and burrows of the forest floor.

The truth was she felt shy, and could never find enough courage to join in. And because she didn't *ask* to play, the others thought she didn't *want* to play – so they never bothered about her. She ended up being left out of everything. "Hi, Sleepyhead!" was the most anyone ever said to her.

Leading a solitary life was very boring. She had nothing to do all day long but follow her instinct for collecting and hoarding. Soft berries and fungi she couldn't resist eating on the spot, and that was why she grew fat, but dry nuts and seeds she stored in the trunk of a huge dead tree that stood at the foot of the mountain. At the bottom of this trunk was a hole hidden by a stone. Much higher up was another hole, and this was where she poked the nuts and seeds she had collected in her dry mouth pouchs.

Since there was always food of one sort or another available on the island, such an enormous store was quite pointless. But filling it occupied her lonely days; growing fatter and fatter, she ate and collected and slept, every day was the same.

When the other squirrels grew tired of playing, which wasn't often, they too would idly store away a bit of food. But their hoards were usually in damp or obvious places: the mice and crows would raid them or sometimes Pig or Porcupine would stumble upon them and that would be that. More often than not the squirrels simply forgot where their stores were hidden, and the nuts and seeds rotted or sprouted when the rains came.

One day, during the cool season, the unsettled weather grew more than usually cool – it grew very cold indeed. The sky over the sea became heavier and greyer by the hour. The finches perched silent in the trees, as if they had some foreboding of disaster.

The cutting wind came first, from the shadow side of the island. The leaves spun, showing their silver undersides. "It's going to rain," said Pig, knowingly; the cold penetrated his bristly fur. He shivered.

The wind increased in strength, the tree tops heaved; fruit and berries fell to the forest floor: *tump, tump* they went as they hit the ground. The squirrels came in from their playing and huddled together underground. How the wind seemed to search and search down their long burrow tunnels.

The gale blew the nuts from the trees and bushes; they fell like hailstones, *putt, putt, putt* against the leaves. Porcupine huddled in his tiny cave; the deer sheltered behind the rocks by the drinking pool, and the air was filled with wind-tossed blossom.

But it wasn't blossom time! These petals were snow-flakes, and now the deer had cold white noses.

Already littered with nuts and berries blown from the trees, the forest floor filled up with snow. Deeper it grew, so that the squirrels' burrows became muffled and dark. And still it snowed. And still the icy wind blew.

"What is it?" said the animals. "What has happened?"

The wind blew all that night. The snow heaped up in drifts around the tree trunks. Even if the squirrels had remembered where their stores lay hidden they could not have got at them.

At first light everyone was cold and hungry. The wind had dropped but the sky hung heavy and grey and the forest lay deep in snow. The branches were bare of food. The monkeys were hungry, the deer were hungry, the mice and finches were hungry. Pig was hungry.

"We're going to die, aren't we?" said Hedgehog to Tortoise. Tortoise felt too cold and slow to answer. He stared out over the endless sea. But it was true, for if the small animals and birds didn't get any food soon they would probably die – some of them that very day.

The squirrels tunnelled desperately in and out of the snow looking for their hidden supplies. They blamed wild pigs and crows for stealing them.

The fat and lonely chipmunk woke cold and hungry like everyone else. Hedgehog's snout came snuffling at her burrow entrance hoping for a snail or worm.

"Good morning," said Hedgehog, "you've missed out on everything as usual."

He told Chipmunk all about the storm and how the cold blossom-like snow now covered everything; he told her how the birds and animals would soon starve to death one by one, beginning with the smallest, which meant mice and squirrels like her. "If you don't believe me, come and see the snow for yourself," said Hedgehog.

Chipmunk, barely awake, followed Hedgehog out of her burrow. It certainly was cold. The snow beneath her paws woke Chipmunk up. "There's no need . . ." she muttered to herself.

"There's no need . . . what?" asked Hedgehog.

"There's no need to starve," said Chipmunk, suddenly bright-eyed. Then she told Hedgehog why.

Hedgehog grew very excited. "Come on," he fussed, "what are we waiting for! Let's go and find this tree of yours."

As they set out for the dead tree at the foot of the mountain, Hedgehog told everyone about Chipmunk's secret store.

"If this is a joke, then it's a very cruel one," said the other squirrels. But they followed her all the same for anything was worth trying.

Soon there was a fluttering and hopping procession of birds and small animals going towards the edge of the forest. Tortoise and Pig had helped to flatten some sort of a path through the deep snow. It wasn't long before they had all gathered at the foot of the tall bleached tree that stood among a jumble of boulders at the bottom of the mountain.

At first Chipmunk couldn't find the stone that blocked the lower hole of her food store. The others helped to clear away the snow. When at last they found it, the stone wouldn't move. Pig swung at it with his tusks; the whole clearing held its breath.

And then the stone spun aside. Out of the hole spurted a wave, a flood, an avalanche of dry nuts, golden seeds and hard-skinned berries. The foot of the tree swarmed with mice and squirrels, jungle fowl and finches while the larger animals waited their turn. There was plenty for everyone. As quickly as they cleared the food from in front of the hole, more flooded out. There was sufficient dried food stored in the height of that huge hollow tree to keep them all going for many days.

Tortoise wasn't keen on wrinkled berries, but he chewed on them patiently and soon he felt better. Pig stuffed himself with nuts; they were his favourite food.

"We've got a lot to thank you for, Chipmunk," chattered the other squirrels. But, as usual, Chipmunk was barely able to say anything and turned away tied up in knots of shyness.

The snow melted in a few days. The sun shone and the forest dried out. The squirrels went to Chipmunk's burrow every morning and asked her to play. On the fourth day she came outside and watched. On the fifth day she joined in.

It never again snowed heavily on Firefly Island, though sometimes in the cool season the top of the mountain shone crisp and white. The rotten tree eventually blew down, but it was quite empty, for Chipmunk never kept a store again – she was too busy playing. And with all the hiding and chasing she became quite thin and nimble.

"What is it like to be dead?" the squirrels asked Tortoise, when he had finished the story about the snow and everyone almost starving to death.

Tortoise watched the ribbon of waves coming up over the sand. He was not sure. "I look at the fallen leaves and shrivelled mosses," he said, "and I see them ever so slowly become earth.

The trees and bushes and plants feed from the earth and we, in turn, feed from them. In this way, the leaves and moss are never lost; they are part of us. How much of me is leaf and moss; how much of me is Tortoise?"

The tide was coming in and frothing around his legs. The squirrels ran further up the beach.

"I cannot see," said Tortoise, puzzled, "exactly where anything begins or ends."

IV
THE UNWELCOME
VISITOR

Firefly Island had been buffeted by many storms, so it was no surprise that Tortoise had stories to tell about the winds and high seas he had seen.

The winds came from far over the ocean and soon disappeared again; but often the seas would leave behind strange things on the sand: shells and oddly shaped branches – and other things that Tortoise didn't understand at all.

"Tell us the story of Big Bottlenose," said the Pelicans.

The story had begun on this very beach, so Tortoise closed his eyes and tried to remember how it had been.

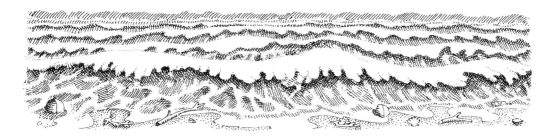

Once there was a tremendous storm. All night the island had been pounded by steep breakers and heaving surf, but by morning the wind had dropped and a watery sun rose over the white sands. There on the beach lay an extra rock, just where the stream ran out of the forest and down to the sea.

The pelicans discovered it first. It was an enormous black boulder, seven times as big as Tortoise.

"But it's not stone at all," said one of the pelicans, looking closer, "it's got two eyes and a mouth." And it had.

"I want to go back in the sea," said the bottlenose whale unhappily. But she was firmly stuck, high up the slope of the beach where huge waves had washed her the night before.

"Why don't you roll and flap down to the sea like we do?" said the seals. But she couldn't. The finches flew into the forest and sounded the alarm: "Come and help, come and help!" they twittered.

All the animals tried to roll the whale back into the water – but, even with Tortoise and the pigs helping, it was hopeless.

"It's so hot," groaned the whale as the sky grew bluer and the sun rose higher. She had to get back into the sea soon or she would die. Everyone thought hard.

Then the monkeys had an idea: "Remember that wall we built across the stream when it was so hot?"

Pig remembered: the monkeys had made a lovely cool pond under the shade of the trees.

"And remember when we broke down the wall?" said one of the monkeys with a smile. They remembered.

The animals set to work at once. On the edge of the forest, where the little stream ran down the sloping sands to the sea, they began to build a dam. The curving wall grew higher, the stream became a pond; it grew deeper and deeper.

Meanwhile, to keep Big Bottlenose cool and moist, the pelicans went back and forth to the sea's edge and scooped up water in their beaks. They poured the water over the whale's back.

"Thank you," she sighed, "that's lovely."

It was a tremendous dam. The monkeys wove rushes and creeper in and out of the tree trunks. They carried branches and rocks to build the wall. Pig shovelled mud and blocked up any gaps with tussocks of grass. Tortoise helped roll the bigger boulders into place. They made sure that the centre of the dam had a weak spot – it was part of the plan.

As the pond filled, its water stretched back into the forest. Before long the dam was as high as it could be and the water started to flow thinly over the top.

"We're ready," said the monkeys. They began to pull out the stones from the centre of the dam. Below the dam lay the stranded whale, and down the slope of the beach lay the sea.

The monkeys took away as many stones as they dared: they were frightened that before they could jump clear, the dam would burst and the flood of water wash them out to sea.

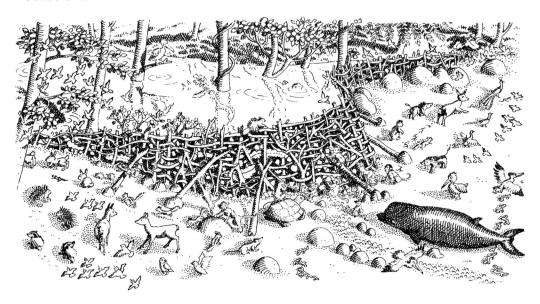

Tortoise tucked in his head and charged at the weakened wall with his heavy shell. It began to give way and water spurted through gaps in the stones. Tortoise took a deep breath and dug his claws firmly into the sand. Would the monkeys' plan work?

With a rumble the dam collapsed. A wall of green water curled down the beach, swirled around the poor hot whale, lifted her up and rolled her down to the waiting sea like a great black log. With a flap of her broad tail she finally pushed herself out from the shallows into the deep waters of the lagoon.

The animals cheered. The whale blew a whoosh of spray from her blow-hole. "Thank you," she called, "thank you. How can I ever repay you!"

Thinking that it would be the last they'd ever see of Big Bottlenose, the animals waved and shouted goodbye.

The bottlenose whale, the twisted logs, the shells and seaweed – they were not all that the sea washed up on the night of the storm.

Clinging desperately to a floating jumble of driftwood came another creature. Only a solitary finch, sleepless on his wind-tossed perch, saw it arrive, but he was unable to follow it in the dark.

After the animals had freed the whale and returned to the cool of the forest, they had a feeling of unease: the finches and chipmunks were puzzled as to why some of their friends were missing. As the day wore on they sensed that something was terribly wrong: there had been strange pouncings in the undergrowth and hidden panic in the lower branches of the trees.

"There's something after us!" the finches sang.

"Yes, something attacked us too!" chattered the squirrels.

A foreign smell hung in the air. A few feathers were found and strange footprints in the wet earth of the forest paths. The deer said they would follow the trail.

It didn't take them long to find the intruder. He was crouching under a bush, a wide smile on his face.

"What do you want?" one of the deer asked him. "Why do you bring fear and trouble to Firefly Island, where do you come from?"

But the cat didn't answer, he only smiled in a knowing, self-satisfied sort of a way. A finch's feather hung from his whiskers.

The deer went back and told Tortoise and the others what they had seen. Pig was furious, his teeth chattered in rage and he set off along the path at a gallop, determined to skewer this strange animal with his tusks. But when Pig arrived and skidded head-over-heels into the bush in a fountain of leaves, the cat sprang gracefully onto a low branch and settled down to cleaning his paws as if nothing had happened.

The animals asked Tortoise what they should do. They had to get rid of the intruder. How awful if one day the trees stood bare of birds; if sunrise and sunset were empty of singing.

"Unless we do something," said Dormouse, "there will be no-one smaller than Porcupine left alive."

"Better to act sooner rather than later," agreed Pig, who was still a bit dazed.

Tortoise turned away and dragged himself down to the sea's edge to think. His head was empty of plans. Why should an intruder have to spoil everything! As Tortoise lay there worrying, a nose and a pair of eyes appeared out of the water. It was Big Bottlenose.

"I thought you were long gone," sighed Tortoise.

"No," replied the whale cheerfully, "your island is as good a place as any to wait for some of my own kind to pass by again. The ocean is a big place to be alone."

"It must be," agreed Tortoise, who suddenly felt lonely too.

"You seem very miserable," said the whale, "what's happened?"

Tortoise told the whale their troubles.

"How did this creature get here?" asked the whale. The others

31

had gathered round Tortoise, but only one bird knew how the cat had arrived.

"I saw," chirruped the finch, "on the night of the storm! It came in with the waves, on a jumble of strange logs."

The whale was thoughtful; it didn't take her long to shape a plan.

"If the creature came from over the ocean," she said, "then that is where we must return it. All we need is a fresh offshore wind and a small, but brave volunteer."

Before she could stop herself, Dormouse opened her mouth: "I'll do it," she squeaked, "I'll do it, really I will."

Nobody slept well that night – and having heard the whale's plan, Dormouse slept worse than any of them. She prayed that by morning there would be a stiff wind blowing in from the sea, and the plan would have to be abandoned.

At first light a silent procession of chipmunks and finches, mice and lizards, hedgehogs, frogs and rabbits – and every other animal and bird smaller than Porcupine – followed Pig to the cave set deep in the rocks by the drinking pool. It was damp and dark inside. Pig and Tortoise stood guard at the entrance. "We're safe here," said the squirrels.

"Maybe," jeered the rabbits, "but who wants to spend the rest of their lives in a mouldy old hole like this."

Tortoise watched the leaves high above the cave entrance. He smiled. The wind was blowing down from the mountain. It blew across the mossy tree tops and on out to sea.

"Dormouse is out there alone," sniffled Pig, "I wonder how she's getting on?"

Dormouse was looking for the cat. The pelicans had flown back and forth over the forest and reported the cat's position. The cat lay asleep in a patch of sunlight not far from the sandy bay. Everything was perfect.

Dormouse crept up to the cat as he slept and pulled one of his whiskers. A big green eye stared at Dormouse. "Oh, sorry to disturb you," squeaked Dormouse, pretending to be horrified, "I thought you were Rabbit." At once she moved off, dragging one of her legs behind her as if she was lame.

The cat, so surprised at what had happened – and so curious to know what this fool of a mouse was up to – held back from catching and killing the dormouse straightaway. The cat had a few questions to put first: "Where is everyone?" he asked, in his slow silky voice, "I woke up hungry this morning, but found the island suddenly empty of anything worth eating – save for one rather dim, lame dormouse, of course!"

"Well, they've gone," shrugged Dormouse.

"Gone? But where?" asked the cat.

"Not telling," replied Dormouse and dragged herself off into the undergrowth.

This mouse was easy to follow and the cat had more questions. He placed a heavy paw on her tail and held her fast.

Dormouse pretended to be terrified. "Oh please don't eat me," she begged. "If you eat me you'll never find the others; I would be your very last meal – my secret would go with me."

"What secret?" said the cat, cautiously.

"The secret of where the others are hiding," said Dormouse.

"Do you mean," said the cat quietly, "that I could find the others? That they haven't gone far?"

Dormouse nodded her head and lowered her eyes. "And you're going to help me, aren't you?" said the cat sweetly.

Dormouse bowed her head as if full of shame. "Follow me," she said, in a whisper.

Still limping, Dormouse led the cat towards the sandy beach at the edge of the forest. Their progress was painfully slow, and the cat grew hungrier by the minute. When it came to crossing the stream they faced a great delay for the cat was terrified of getting his fur wet and Dormouse, with her pretend bad leg, made a show of being unable to leap or climb over anything. In the end Dormouse hung on to the cat's back as it sprang across a narrow stretch of water downstream.

Now they were on the beach, the sand hot on Dormouse's pink feet. She led the cat to the very edge of the sea, where rounded boulders and spits of sand jutted out into the deep water. A warm wind from the forest ruffled the surface of the lagoon so that it was difficult to see the shell-strewn bottom easily.

Dormouse limped out to the very end of a jetty of sand, and with a sigh she slumped down in the shade of a large trunk of driftwood washed up by the tide.

"I don't see anything at all," said the cat, joining Dormouse. He was determined the mouse shouldn't slip away but he was nervous of the deep water lapping on three sides of them.

"Don't panic," said Dormouse, with another little sigh, "have a rest, relax. We're very close now." But truthfully she already had the cat just where she wanted him.

The cat could not relax. Water made him jittery. And hadn't he felt something of a tremor in the sand and rocks beneath him? Yes, there it was again!

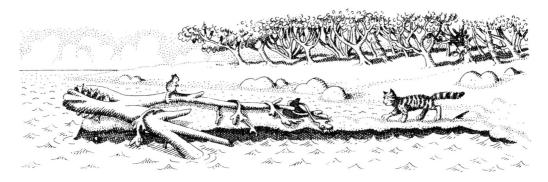

It was too late to run away. At that moment Big Bottlenose propelled herself out into the lagoon, with the cat, the log, and Dormouse balanced on the patch of her back which remained clear of the water. Most of the sand and seaweed with which the pelicans had disguised her was washed away.

Dormouse waved goodbye to the cat and then threw herself into the water. A sharp-eyed pelican, who knew the whale's plan, landed at once on the waves beside Dormouse and scooped up the sodden little creature in its beak. Big Bottlenose, meanwhile, sank lower and lower in the water so that the cat had no choice but to jump onto the log and hold on.

The whale dived into the glassy blue depths and away. There was the cat, dry but alone. The pelicans, who were kind birds, had wedged a wad of fresh fish into a hole in the log, so that the cat would not starve.

The wind blew the log further and further from Firefly Island, until, to the animals watching from the beach, it became only a black speck on the wide turquoise sea. And then it was gone.

Everyone congratulated Dormouse as she dried herself on a hot rock. They had come rushing from the cave as soon as they'd heard from the pelicans that the cat was adrift on the log. But where was Big Bottlenose? They had not had a chance to thank her.

"Where had she gone?" the finches asked Tortoise, when he had finished the story. But Tortoise didn't know. He wondered what it was like to live in such emptiness. Firefly Island was surely the best, the only place to be.

V
THE CAVE OF
THE COLD WIND

One evening, when the animals of Firefly Island had gathered on the beach to hear Tortoise's stories, somebody mentioned Bear.

"This has been just the sort of hot and horrible day that Bear would have hated," grumbled Wild Pig, rolling in the damp sand.

"Bear?" asked some of the younger animals, puzzled. "Who is Bear? What is Bear?"

Tortoise was one of the few animals old enough to remember Bear. "Bear is no longer with us," said Tortoise. "He is here on Firefly Island but we don't see him."

"Tortoise is telling us, in a gentle way, that Bear is dead," said one of the rabbits.

"No, I am sure Bear is not dead," Tortoise replied quickly, glancing up at the steep mountain that stood at the centre of their island. "If ever you could find the Cave of the Cold Wind, then I am certain you would find Bear, too."

The animals stared at the faraway mountain rising above the trees. Its jagged ridge of honey-coloured rock came straight out of the sea on one side of the island, reached a sharp summit in the middle, and then fell back steeply into the sea on the other side. Goats lived on its lower slopes; their hooves had worn giddy little paths between the ledges where they fed and the caves where they sheltered. Above them was high country that belonged only to the eagles. No grass or scrub grew there. Vicious winds blew over the sharp ridge; the air was thin and cold and bare rock sparkled with frost. The mountain was a barrier to whatever lay beyond.

"The mountain has so many caves," sang the finches, suddenly curious to see Bear. "Which is the special cave where Bear lives? Which is the Cave of the Cold Wind?"

"You won't find Bear," grunted the rabbits, "the caves are hot and airless and they stink of goat droppings. No-one would want to live up there: not even this bear, whoever or whatever he is."

But Tortoise was not listening to the finches or rabbits. Thinking of Bear had reminded him of a terrible time on Firefly Island long, long ago.

"If it had not been for Bear," he said quietly, "I think that none of us would be here this evening."

A sudden hush fell upon the animals.

"Once," said Tortoise, "the sun shone like it did today. But it shone hard and hot every day, for countless days. We enjoyed it for a while: such cascades of flowers there were; such smells from the dry forest floor; such warm comfortable nights. But the rains that usually come after the blossom has fallen did not arrive. No clouds billowed up over the horizon. The day of the shortest shadow came and went; and still it had not rained.

"The precious Rizzleberry fruit hung hard and shrivelled as pink seashells and across every green leaf in the forest crept a bitter brown stain of dryness. The smaller streams ran dry and their muddy bottoms opened up into deep cracks. The waterfalls that had once roared white and achingly cold became silent: only thin trickles of tepid water snaked over their slimy rocks. The bog where the frogs lived turned slowly into a bowl of dust. Those were bad times," sighed Tortoise, "terrible times for all of us. But especially bad for Bear."

"Why?" asked the rabbits.

"Because Bear was a big animal," Tortoise replied, "and his fur was thick and black, and quite soon he was dreadfully hot and uncomfortable. Normally he would have lain blissfully beneath one of the waterfalls or swum in a pond deep in the forest. But it wasn't long before the only fresh water left on the island was a little dribble running from the foot of the cliffs into the drinking pool."

"Why didn't he go for a swim in the sea?" asked one of the rabbits.

"Because," said Tortoise, "the salt water made Bear's skin itch, and when it dried, his fur stood up fluffier than ever. Poor Bear was miserable, he lay in the shade by the drinking pool with his chin on his paws and dreamed all day and all night of slipping down the pebbly edge into the clear cool water."

"Why didn't he just jump in?" asked the rabbit.

"The pool was for drinking, not for swimming in," Tortoise replied. "During the day I stayed on guard. The animals had to queue up to drink; I was there to make sure nobody stirred up the mud or drank more than they needed." Just telling the animals about it all made Tortoise's mouth feel terribly dry.

As the drought worsened, the animals became very frightened. Was this the end? Had it come so soon? They had often grumbled or complained about their ordinary lives but now they seemed precious and wonderful. They didn't want to die.

Bear felt more uncomfortable than afraid. One night, hot and sticky, he could put up with it no longer. Making sure that everyone was fast asleep, he padded delicately to the edge of the pool and as quietly as possible, nose first, he slid into the moon's perfect reflection.

Ah! how deliciously cool it was, what a relief; his hot sweaty fur soaked to its roots at last. He lay on his back looking up at the firefly stars, determined not to worry about tomorrow. Who would ever know he had done this? He could take a secret swim every night. It was a lovely thought.

But the next day, when the animals lined up and took their turns to drink, there was uproar.

"Ugh! the water's bad!" said Badger.

"It's revolting," said the monkeys.

"It tastes of damp fur," said Wild Pig.

"It tastes of *Bear*!" said Porcupine.

"Oh Bear! How could you do such a thing," cried all the animals together.

They were furious. They shouted at Bear; they insulted him; they promised never ever to forgive him.

Bear was a bit taken aback: was it such a terrible thing that he had done?

"We don't want you any more," said the other animals, "we never want to see you again."

There is no feeling so awful as when everybody hates you. Even in the hot dry air Bear's eyes became rather moist. He turned his back on them all and lumbered off into the forest. Their hate followed him like a smell; like a swarm of angry honey-bees. He wanted to get as far away as possible from their cross faces and dislike. He wanted to find a place where he would not be disturbed.

Bear travelled right through the forest until he reached the great wall of Firefly Mountain. One of those caves up there would be a good place to hide, he thought, as he set off up a narrow path made by the goats. Soon he was high above the forest. He didn't care if he fell. His clumsy paws sent stones clattering down into the tree tops.

But when he reached the caves they were hot and smelly, so Bear climbed higher and higher always hoping he might find a better one.

And he did.

One of the caves was lovely and cool. Good, thought Bear in his misery, I shall find the back of the cave and curl up in a big ball and go to sleep – and with any luck I shall never wake up again.

But this cave ran deep and dark into the mountain and Bear could not find the back of it. There were alcoves and smaller caves leading off the main passageway but these smelt stale and uninviting. A cold breeze ruffled Bear's fur, he was sure he could smell trees and ferns. His black nose led him on. Normally, Bear might have been afraid in such complete darkness, but though he could see nothing, the wind blowing through the cave grew sweeter and cooler. He could smell wet moss now, and wasn't that the roar of the sea?

A faint light began to show on the rock walls of the passageway; and then round a bend, perhaps a thousand paw-lengths away, Bear saw a tiny circle of daylight.

The cave had narrowed now so that Bear's bottom brushed the roof and sides. Nearer and nearer came the end of the tunnel and then suddenly he was out in the open.

Bear couldn't believe what he saw: below him a steep green landscape of stunted bushes and white waterfalls led away down the mountainside to the tree tops of a dark forest. And curved around the edge of the forest was the sea.

Bear had come *through* the mountain; he had found a secret way. He was now the other side of Firefly Island.

The ledges of rock beside him were cushioned with old snow. The sun never reached this face of the mountain nor even the forest below. The plants and trees were different here: they liked the coolness and the shade – just like I do, thought Bear happily. He plunged his muzzle into an icy stream and took a long, long drink. Silver fish darted in the pools and larger fish leapt the waterfalls. The shrubs were heavy with ripe berries; some bitter and some sweet. This is the place for me, thought Bear, the perfect place.

He had just set off down the mountainside to enjoy his new world when suddenly he remembered the other animals – they were back there, on the other side, baked and blistered and without water. Bear made up his mind to forget them all; they had not forgiven him so why should he forgive them. Bear felt quite indignant.

But the memory of the parched animals followed him, like the shadow of a horrible bird. He felt uncomfortable and ugly inside. The memory stopped him enjoying the dew-wet berries and the clouds of cool mountain mist. Remembering the thirsty animals spoiled everything – and Bear realised that it always would. So he turned around and headed back up the slope to the small dark mouth of his secret cave.

The next day, back at the empty drinking pool, Lizard and a few of the chipmunks were licking the last damp patches of mud to cool their tongues. The other animals lay around the pool in what shade remained. The sky was clear and cloudless – there was no hope of rain. The end of everything seemed near.

And then Bear crashed through the bushes scattering flocks of tiny birds. "Where's Tortoise?" he demanded. "Where are Badger and Pig? I've got some important news."

"Oh, Bear," said Pig, with a mean sneer in his voice, "nice to see you again, Bear. Have a swim, we really don't mind. Go on, enjoy yourself."

Bear looked at the empty drinking pool and the circle of miserable animals. "I've got something very important to say," Bear growled and he told them what he had found.

The animals followed Bear up the zig-zag of the stony goat tracks. First the deer and then Coati; then Pig and the porcupines; then the monkeys and Lizard and Grass Snake. The pelicans and partridges followed, and a long way behind struggled the rabbits, dormice, squirrels and a fluttering of finches.

Pig felt giddy under the glare of the sun. Sometimes his hind hooves slipped off the edge of the narrow path and kicked for a moment in thin air. He muttered to himself, "If this is some sort of cruel joke of yours, Bear, I will never, ever . . ." But Pig could not think of anything sufficiently awful with which to threaten Bear: things couldn't get worse than they already were.

"How will you know which cave it is?" panted Porcupine.

"I scratched the rock outside with my claws," said Bear. "I'll know which cave it is when I get there."

And he did.

Here were the claw marks, and here the cold wind blew. There was a lot of bumping of noses and pulling of tails along the dark passage of Bear's cave. Nobody wanted to lose touch with those in front. Only Mole felt completely at home. The squeaks, grunts and chattering of the animals echoed strangely up and down the cave.

The tunnel narrowed so that the deer had to lower their heads. And then a glimmer of light glistened on the damp rock, and rounding a corner the animals saw a far-off circle of sky.

A booming, scraping sound in the tunnel behind them alarmed the finches. "Quick!" they cried out. "The roof's falling in!" But the noise didn't come again and the animals hurried on towards the daylight.

Then, there they were, tumbling from the cave mouth out into Bear's secret country. How wonderful the water tasted, how sweet the berries.

"Thank you, Bear, thank you, Bear!"

The finches pecked at his ears in gratitude, the dormice jumped up and down on his paws. Bear enjoyed being a hero. Everyone thanked him; everyone except the pelicans who were busy flying from the stream to the cave and back again. Bear wondered what errand they were on.

High above the summit of the mountain soared two eagles.

"You knew all this water was here," shouted the monkeys, "and yet you never told us. How could you not tell us?"

But the eagles, as always, gave no hint that they had heard.

Soon night shadowed the mountain. It was very cold. A burr of frost crisped the edge of each leaf and blade of grass; stones by the stream's edge became slippery with ice. Bear felt warm enough with his thick coat but the other animals were chilled.

They huddled around him to keep warm; the finches and partridges fluffed up their feathers; the squirrels and dormice burrowed deep into Bear's fur. The deer browsed patiently, their breath hanging like mist in the frosty air. Nobody wanted to sleep next to Porcupine. Pig grunted in his sleep and his little hooves twitched as – in his dreams – he ran from a pack of angry bears.

The next day the animals moved down the mountain and into the dark green woods. It was warmer here and the forest floor was springy and brown. The tall trees had needle-like leaves, the berries on the bushes were large and tough; the river crashed powerful and white between huge rounded boulders. It was big country, best suited to big animals. Bear felt completely at home but the other animals did not.

Every day, Bear sent one of the energetic monkeys to look over the other side of the mountain to see if it had rained yet. For a long time they were disappointed, but one evening a monkey came back and said he had seen great clouds boiling up on the far horizon; and a warm moist wind blew from that direction, too.

The next day the monkey bounded down the mountainside, tripping and rolling over in his excitement. He told them that the far-off clouds had now gathered low over the island on the other side and raindrops as big as rizzleberries drummed from leaf to leaf; the streams ran muddy but full, and already the brown clearings had sprouted a green haze of new shoots. The drought was over and it was time for the animals to go home.

But Bear was staying. He was happy here: out of his misery had come great contentment. So he said his goodbyes, one by one.

"Did you say goodbye?" asked one of the rabbits when Tortoise had finished telling the story of Bear. Tortoise seemed uncomfortable; he didn't reply.

"We were always told," said the rabbit, "that there was nothing but sea and sky the other side of the mountain. How wonderful to have actually *been* there. You really do know everything, Tortoise."

But Tortoise looked rather embarrassed. "I didn't say goodbye to Bear," he confessed, "though I wish I had. There was a reason why I didn't."

"What was the reason?" asked Rabbit.

Tortoise cleared his throat. "Do you remember I told you how the finches heard a scraping noise and they thought the roof of the cave was collapsing? Well, the tunnel grew narrower and narrower as it neared the other side . . ." Tortoise paused for a moment, " . . . and I got stuck!"

The animals on the beach couldn't help laughing, but Tortoise didn't mind. "That was why the pelicans were flying up to Bear's cave with beaksful of freshwater – I was terribly thirsty."

"Did you ever get unstuck?" asked another rabbit.

Tortoise smiled. "Of course I did. But it wasn't very funny at the time. The tunnel was full of animals who had said goodbye to Bear, and I was blocking their way. I don't go very fast when I'm going forwards, but I almost never have reason to go backwards: I was very out of practice."

"I would love to have seen Bear," sighed the rabbit, "I wonder if he's still there."

"I'm sure he is," said Tortoise cheerfully. "I'm sure he's very happy."

The sky slowly turned red and then a deep dark blue as day

disappeared over the sea. That night, as Tortoise slept beneath the rustling leaves on the edge of the forest, he dreamed of Bear. And in his dream, Bear hugged Tortoise with his warm leathery paws: a great big hug that was both 'goodbye' and 'hello'; a hug that told Tortoise everything was going well.

VI
King Badger

At the end of one hot and sultry day, as the animals gathered together on the beach, a distant rumble filled the sky: a sound like a huge tortoise's shell being scraped against a boulder. The clouds far over the sea lit up with flashes of white light.

"There's a storm brewing," said Wild Pig, knowingly. The smaller animals began to get nervous and fidgety.

"Don't be afraid," said Tortoise calmly. "In all my life I have only known thunder and lightning hurt one animal – and even then, not very seriously."

"Tell us about it, Tortoise," the animals said, "we are all listening."

"All except Badger," said the rabbits, "he's gone off somewhere."

"In the circumstances that is not surprising," Tortoise said with a smile, "for in fact my story is all about Badger."

Peacock was partly to blame for what happened to Badger.

Peacock was moulting and very worried about losing his good looks. One morning he stopped Badger in his tracks. "Tell me I'm still beautiful," he begged, "all my feathers are falling out."

"Don't worry, you look quite splendid," said Badger, who like all badgers was terribly short-sighted; he was the last person Peacock should have gone to for an opinion.

Peacock, feeling generous in his new hope, began to flatter Badger, "Well, you yourself are an unusually handsome badger, you know."

"Thank you," said Badger, thoughtfully. He'd never bothered very much with his appearance and in fact he was a rather flea-ridden bramble-torn specimen. But from that day on, a feeling of being superior began to grow in Badger. He became discontented with the noise and bustle of family life; of sleeping below ground in a cramped hole with his argumentative brothers and sisters. I am too good for all this, he thought, I want to be free of the drudgery of being an ordinary badger. In his determination to be something special, Badger left home.

He went first of all to visit a sleek and beautiful badger who lived on the other side of the forest. For a long time Badger had only dreamed of daring to ask her to be his mate: now he felt both brave enough and handsome enough. He was a bit puzzled when she refused even to look at him. Never mind, thought Badger, I will try again another day when my appearance has improved still further.

But he didn't manage very well on his own. He was cold at night and whenever it rained he got soaked through. His ragged unkempt claws were in too poor a condition for him to dig a nice dry burrow all by himself. He wasn't even very good at snouting for worms and roots. Badger gradually fell into a dreadful state.

One day, bumbling along a path through the undergrowth, Badger bumped into a rabbit crying her eyes out. "What's the matter?" he asked.

"The deer are kicking us off the Big Clearing," sniffed the rabbit. "It has the sweetest, richest grass and we've always been allowed to graze there and now they say we can't."

In general the badgers and the rabbits didn't get on together, but Badger was glad of company: even miserable company was better than none at all. "Come along," he said reassuringly, "we'll go and sort it out."

So they found the Big Clearing and peered out from under the bushes to see what was going on. It was true: whenever a rabbit hopped out of the circle of trees onto the grass, the deer would push it away with their foreheads or even kick out with their small black hooves. They were being very possessive about the grazing.

Badger ruffled up his fur so as to look especially fierce. "You big bullies," he growled, rushing out into the open, "why not pick on somebody your own size." He ran in wild circles, grunting and grumbling, nipping at their heels. The deer were terrified and bounded off into the shadows of the trees not knowing what had attacked them.

Badger glowed with pride. He was a hero. The rabbits said they couldn't think of any way to thank him. Badger couldn't think of anything either. But then the rabbit who had been in tears found a large juicy worm and brought it to Badger as a present. That one worm was the beginning of all the trouble that followed.

"Thank you," said Badger, pleasantly surprised, "I am very fond of worms," and it was a delicious worm too. Badger thought the rabbits ought to know what else he liked. "The occasional beetle or slug would be very welcome," he added, "and fruit and berries too, when they are in season."

And that is how it all began. There were so many rabbits that it was really no bother supplying one solitary badger.

Badger grew fatter and his unused claws grew longer. He protected the rabbits with the occasional display of fierceness. He even chased the deer from clearings where the rabbits had never normally been allowed to graze. But in general his life was one of ease.

Badger lived down the rabbit burrows with the rabbits, but he couldn't really get used to their smell, or to being squashed by dozens of baby rabbits who scratched and kicked out with their back legs as they slept.

When he visited the sleek badger he loved and told her of his easy life and the wonderful food provided for him, she just sniffed the air and said that he smelled like a rabbit.

"You are turning into a Babbit or a Radger," one of her friends said to Badger with a laugh. Badger felt dreadfully hurt.

"I don't suppose you would dig me a burrow of my own?" Badger asked the rabbits eventually. They agreed, but one or two of them were a bit grumpy at having to excavate such a large hole. It took them several days and Badger found he was losing patience. "If you don't dig a little harder," he whispered to the rabbit who had complained the most, "then I shall come down your burrow one night and give you a jolly good bite."

Badger's hole was quickly finished. But he wasn't very comfortable. With no mate or brothers and sisters to groom him, Badger soon became plagued by fleas. As he lay awake itching and scratching he blamed the rabbits. After only a few days, Badger left his new hole for good.

"I'm going to sleep above ground from now on," he informed the rabbits. "I want you to build me a canopy to keep the rain and the sun off, and I also want you to bring me enough dried grass so that I can have a fresh bed every day." There's nothing like good hygiene to get rid of fleas, thought Badger.

The rabbits were fed up. "If, as well as gathering a badgerful of worms, we have to spend all our day nipping off blades of grass and drying it in the sun and fluffing it up into a nice bed for Badger, then we're going to starve. We need some help."

And because they had been ill-used by Badger, they very quickly thought of a way to get what they needed by ill-treating somebody else. Some of the tougher rabbits set off through the forest in gangs searching for partridges. The partridges nested on the ground and they were easy for rabbits to find.

"You're very good at building nests," said the rabbits, "we need lots of dry grass to make Badger a bed, and we hope that you will collect some for us."

"And if we don't?" said the partridges, surprised.

"If you don't," said the rabbits darkly, "Badger will give us a bite and we in turn will come and stamp on your eggs."

The partridges drew in their breath with a quivering sound.

"And there's another thing that Badger wants," said the rabbits, "something that we have neither the skill nor the time to arrange."

"What's that?" asked the partridges.

"A nice canopy to shield Badger from the hot sun and the rain."

"But we can't build canopies," protested the partridges.

"That," smirked the rabbits, "is your problem." And they hopped away back to their burrows.

So the partridges, bullied by the rabbits, soon hatched a plan that involved bullying someone else. "We can't tie poles together with creeper and build Badger a tent," they agreed, "but we do know someone who can."

And the partridges, in a great whirring of wings, went to visit the monkeys. Flying together in one large flock made them feel quite brave.

"We need your help," they explained to the monkeys. "We can do the grass collecting, and carry it to the rabbits, but we can't do the building work."

"And why should we do it?" shouted the monkeys, laughing rudely. "We don't owe Badger anything."

There was quite a long silence before one of the partridges swallowed hard and hopped to a branch nearer the monkeys. "If you don't build the shelter for Badger," said the partridge, "we will peck a little hole in each and every young piece of fruit in the forest and they will rot before they ever have a chance to ripen."

"But we would starve if all the fruit went bad!" cried the monkeys. "This *is* a joke, isn't it? Is it to pay us back for some harmless trick we played on you in the past and have long since forgotten? If that's so, then we're sorry. You know we never mean anyone any harm."

"We're sorry too," said the partridge, "but it's no joke; we have no choice. And neither have you."

So the monkeys built Badger his beautiful tent. They tied branches together and wove wall panels out of rushes. They lashed thick leaves to the roof, all in neat rows, so that water would run off the edges when it rained. Each day the partridges collected beaksful of dry grass for Badger's bed, and the rabbits dug deep holes in their search for the juicy roots and fine fat worms that Badger demanded for his breakfast.

On sunny days, even under the shade of his canopy, Badger said he felt too hot. He asked the monkeys to fan him with large water lily leaves, and, though the monkeys took it in turns, their thin arms soon ached with all the flapping. It wasn't long before they, with some threat or other, bullied the finches and hummingbirds into fanning Badger for them with their little wings.

"My house still smells of rabbits," complained Badger, so the monkeys decorated it daily with the brightest and sweetest smelling flowers they could find. Badger was very comfortable, but the other animals were miserable. His power had spread across the island like a disease. Fear was making the animals mean. It was easier now to be on Badger's side than not to be. It was better to accept the tasks forced on one than to refuse.

One day Badger decided he wanted to move house. "There is a place I like by the drinking pool," said Badger. "It has good shade and a nice cool wind blows off the sea. And best of all, the Rizzleberry tree will be growing right outside my door."

So the monkeys had to build Badger a bigger and better home on his chosen patch of grass; and when they had finished decorating it with jasmine and honeysuckle – and the partridges had heaped up a bed of fluffy grasses and the rabbits had fetched him leaves heaped with grubs and worms – then, Badger was almost satisfied. But not quite.

"Bring me that glossy badger from the other side of the forest," he ordered, "so that she can see just how much I have improved. Once I was nothing and now I am king!"

The finches groomed him, the rabbits polished his hideously long claws, the hummingbirds fanned him and the monkeys brought rare blue flowers to carpet his doorway.

But when the beautiful badger was brought unwillingly before him, she had nothing encouraging to say. "I am sorry for you," she whispered, "you have everything you want and yet you are further now from being a true badger than ever you were."

Badger shrugged his shoulders when she had gone. "Who cares," he grunted. But deep down he did care.

To be fair, Badger didn't really see how much his luxury was based on the misery of others. He didn't see all the whispering and suspicion, the bullying and threats. He didn't realise what a monster he had become. For him life was good. In the heat of the day he could swim in the drinking pool; and what if it tasted ever so slightly of Badger – it didn't matter breaking the rules: *he* made the rules now.

Honeycomb, thought Badger, as he lay on his back one day listening to the distant waves breaking on the sand, a nice dripping honeycomb would make life better than good – it would make life perfect.

So Badger demanded that the rabbits bring him honeycomb for his tea. The rabbits asked the partridges, the partridges asked the monkeys and the monkeys decided that scooping honeycomb out of hollow tree trunks and getting stung was something they really did not want to do.

"We'll get Coati to do it," they agreed. So they found Coati blissfully asleep under a moonberry bush, and they woke him up rudely and told him to bring a honeycomb to Badger's palace by tea time, without fail.

"And if I don't?" asked Coati.

"If you don't, we will make life unbearable for you," said the monkeys. "Whenever you go to sleep we will drop nuts on you and wake you up; and on the odd occasion when we *do* allow you to sleep, we'll dribble juice from the sticky-fruit all over your fur so that the wasps and bees come and pester you."

"Why have you become so horrible all of a sudden?" Coati asked.

The monkeys had no answer; they could not look Coati in the face. "Don't forget," their voices echoed, as they swung away through the branches. "Tea time, Badger's palace – or else!"

And so it was that a miserable Coati came to see Tortoise. Coati's nose and eyelids were all bumpy with bee stings.

"Something has to be done," nodded Tortoise when he'd listened to Coati's story. Tortoise went to visit Badger in his beautiful palace. The flowering Rizzleberry tree was heavy with finches and hummingbirds waiting their turn to cool King Badger.

"This has got to stop," said Tortoise gruffly when he reached Badger's dazzling doorway, "this is not the way things are meant to be."

"What you really mean," snorted Badger, "is that you don't like being an ordinary tortoise again. You would have liked to have stayed in charge for ever."

"It doesn't matter who's in charge," said Tortoise. "What matters is that everybody is unhappy. If Big Bottlenose were to visit our island today, he wouldn't recognise it – it's a changed place and changed for the worse."

"Nobody else is complaining," said Badger rudely.

"No one else dares complain," snapped Tortoise.

"It looks as though you are intent on spoiling things," sighed Badger. "Roll Tortoise over!" he shouted suddenly to the monkeys, "and take him away and leave him on the beach on his back."

The monkeys hesitated. Birdsong in the forest died away. There was a long, long pause. The only sound was the sea breaking on the rocks in the lagoon. It was as if the whole island held its breath. Was Badger's power terrible enough to do even this?

"It won't take long," said Badger encouragingly, "we'll soon be able to forget all about him."

And so the monkeys swarmed over Tortoise shouting and jeering to give themselves courage. They rocked him onto the back of his shell and slid him away between the thin trees and out onto the baking sand.

If Tortoise had lain upside down in the sun very long he would have died. But he was lucky. Great boulders of purple cloud had been gathering out over the sea and a cold wind now heaved in the trees. The sun was swallowed up by the clouds and the wind grew stronger still. Drops of rain as big as frog's eyes drummed on Tortoise's underside. The rain beat on the roof of Badger's palace too.

"Hold on to the corner posts," Badger shrieked at the monkeys, "you haven't built it strong enough, you idiots; the whole thing is going to take off!"

The little birds from the Rizzleberry tree scattered into low-lying bushes. The sky was split by a jagged flash of lightning; the crash and rumble of it followed a second later. The monkeys let go of Badger's palace and fled into the trees. The rabbits dived for their burrows and the partridges scuttled away to protect their nests. Badger was left all alone in the storm.

The next blinding finger of lightning cracked out of the black sky and stabbed right through the roof of Badger's palace into the earth. Badger had been so close to the lightning-bolt that every hair on his body was singed clean away. He ran from under the collapsing canopy of poles and leaves and out through the doorway of spoiled flowers. Deafened by the thunder, and pink and smooth as a newborn piglet, galloped poor ridiculous Badger. Behind him, his bed of dried grass had caught alight and the whole of his palace was ablaze – his power, and his life, in ruins.

"Who turned you back over?" asked the animals when Tortoise finished his story about Badger.

"The monkeys did; with many apologies," smiled Tortoise. "There was much forgiving to be done on our island that night."

"And what about Badger?" asked Pig, looking anxiously up at the dark clouds.

"He grew a new coat after a while," said Tortoise, "an especially fine one as luck would have it. And he was glad to enjoy the ordinary pleasures of being an ordinary badger. As for the sleek and beautiful badger: well, eventually she agreed to be his mate and they dug themselves a really deep burrow on the edge of the clearing. You won't see old Badger much, he keeps himself to himself, especially on a night like this."

Spots of rain began to darken the sand and the animals drifted back into the forest one by one. There was another flash and growl from far over the sea. Tortoise secretly hated thunderstorms – they were beyond his understanding – but he didn't want the other animals to know that he, their leader, was afraid.

I shall tuck in my head and legs and pretend I am a boulder on the beach, he thought, and then the thunder will not notice me.

But in the end the storm passed harmlessly by, at a great distance. And Tortoise fell deeply asleep and woke the next morning, brave and refreshed.

VII
THE RIZZLEBERRY WAR

"Why do the goats live high up the mountain?" asked one of the young deer as Tortoise sat on the beach telling them stories. "It is so dry and steep up there and bare of anything to eat except thorn bushes."

"The goats are different to us," said Tortoise, "they don't think the same way as we do; they live their lives by different rules."

"Do they ever come down?" asked the deer.

"No," said Tortoise, "they have been up there ever since the Rizzleberry War."

"The Rizzleberry War?" said the deer. "What was that?"

"Give me a moment to gather my memories," said Tortoise, "and I will tell you . . ." And he tried to remember exactly what had happened.

The famous Rizzleberry tree stood on the small strip of grass that grew between the edge of the drinking pool and the steep cliffs of Firefly Mountain. Its twisted trunk threw out many branches: a few of these touched the water and one or two brushed against the rock face. In the blossom season the tree was covered in a dense speckling of small pink flowers. The bees and moths came then, hungry for the nectar in the flowers. And while they were busy in and out the sweet blossom, they carried on their furry backs – without knowing it – the pollen from the male flowers to the female flowers. And where the pollen mingled, there the fruit of the Rizzleberry tree had its first tiny beginnings.

And what a fruit it was! Wonderfully cool even on the hottest day, it burst on your tongue, fizzy, fruity, slightly sweet. There was no taste so fantastic as a ripe Rizzleberry.

But there was a long time to wait between the blossoming and the fruiting, and each year the Rizzleberry tree carried only one harvest of berries. You would think that with so many fruit-eating creatures on Firefly Island, the Rizzleberry tree would be stripped of its berries before they had a chance to ripen. But of all the trees this tree was considered above any ordinary sort of greed. It was a rule, the most important rule on Firefly Island, that the berries were left on the branches until the longest day of the year when the shadow of Eagle Rock lay at its shortest. On that day the animals held a race from one side of the island to the other: and the winner had the first glorious picking of the Rizzleberries.

While the fruit ripened, the animals and birds disciplined themselves not even to look up at the Rizzleberry tree; the temptation to steal might be too great to resist. The animals came to the drinking pool with their eyes lowered, they drank and then they left. That anyone would ever steal the Rizzleberries was quite unthinkable – the Rizzleberry tree was a symbol of the animals' trust of one another.

One year, around the time of the longest day, the monkeys went as usual to measure the length of the shadow on the cliff face. Today the shadow was very short; the day of the race was very near.

In their excitement the monkeys couldn't help glancing down at the drinking pool and at the green haze of the Rizzleberry tree. But wait a moment: it shouldn't be green at all! It should be *red*. Red with ripe berries.

The monkeys sounded the alarm. Somebody had stripped the Rizzleberry tree of its fruit. It wasn't long before all the animals had gathered under the tree to try and work out what had happened. The berries were gone and somebody was to blame.

"It wasn't us," cried the rabbits. "Whoever saw a rabbit climb a tree! You know we need someone to shake the tree for us so that the fruit drops to the ground."

"It wasn't us," said the deer. "We've been over the far side of the island for two days."

"Maybe," said Pig suspiciously, "but how do we know exactly when the fruit was stolen: it might have been several days ago."

"It wasn't us," protested the finches. "You'd know if we'd stolen the berries by the colour of our droppings."

"Well, it certainly wasn't me," said Pig indignantly, "you'd see my hoof marks on the bark."

"Hush, all of you," said Tortoise. "Now think carefully. Does anyone remember the last time they saw berries on the tree?"

There was a long silence. Nobody seemed able to remember.

The truth was there had never *been* any berries on the Rizzleberry tree that year – and for a very good reason. In the blossom season, Badger's palace had stood right beside the tree; the finches had crowded onto the branches while they waited to fan Badger, and whenever a bee or a moth had come anywhere near the blossom they had pecked at it or gobbled it up.

The pollen had not been carried from flower to flower; the fruit had never even begun to grow. And when the finches left the tree during the thunderstorm, heavy raindrops had knocked the blossom to the ground.

The great race that summer was a dull event; nobody tried very hard and – without a prize waiting at the finish – who could blame them. But the next year when the tree was once again heavy with blossom, all their old suspicions returned.

"We are not going to allow the thief to strike again," said Pig one day. "From now on I am going to keep guard right under the tree until the day of the great race itself."

"Don't be silly," said Tortoise, "you've got to sleep and eat; you can't manage on your own."

"Anyway, how do we know Pig won't steal the berries?" said the deer. "We've as much right to guard the tree as he has."

Tortoise sighed. "Pig can guard the tree during the day," he said, "and you can guard the tree at night. If anything happens to the berries we will know who's responsible."

While the tree was still in blossom, the other animals were content to leave it up to Pig and the deer to keep guard – after all, it wasn't a very satisfying job – but as the first hard green beginnings of fruit appeared, all the animals began to take a closer interest.

"Perhaps we wouldn't know if Pig or the deer were stealing the fruit," said Porcupine. "If they just took small amounts each time they were on guard nobody would notice; the tree would look the same."

"Quite so," said Lizard. "I'm going to guard the deer to make sure they keep their noses out of the branches at night."

"And I am going to guard Pig," said Porcupine, "to make sure he isn't tempted into the occasional nibble."

For a while the other animals considered the Rizzleberry tree to be safe. They didn't envy the guards their long hours of duty. But after the rains, when the green berries began to swell and turn pink, the animals' mistrust of each other grew fast.

"How do we know that the deer and Lizard might not come to an agreement to enjoy a little bit of fruit in secret and then promise not to give each other away? Pig and Porcupine might do the same."

"In that case we are going to guard Lizard and the deer," said the dormice.

"And we are going to keep a careful eye on Pig and Porcupine," said the squirrels.

"This is ridiculous," said Tortoise, "no good can come of it all. Let's go home peacefully."

But the animals ignored him: they were too busy expecting the very worst of each other. They quickly divided into two sides; the daytime guards and the night-time guards.

The riper the fruit became, the more tense and suspicious each side grew of the other.

"What if Pig's army suddenly agree to share out the fruit among themselves," whispered the deer, "they could strip the tree bare in less than a day."

"Don't worry," said Lizard, "we will make sure there are enough of us to stop them."

Pig's followers were saying much the same thing about the deer's army.

"If they really stuffed themselves," warned Porcupine, "they could eat all the berries in one night."

"Maybe," said Pig, "but our side will be strong enough to re-capture the tree at the first sign of any trouble."

Each army was eager to get the support of as many animals as possible. Soon there were very few creatures on Firefly Island who had not joined one side or the other.

Pig even went and asked the goats to join his army – though they were usually considered too stupid to be of any help over anything. But the goats wouldn't answer Pig, they just stared at him with their indignant faraway eyes.

The tree grew riper each day. One evening, Tortoise went to the drinking pool and called the animals together.

"I'm very worried," he said. "No good can come of us getting ready to fight each other. Something terrible will happen if we don't sort this out soon."

"What do you suggest then," said Pig crossly, "that we all go back to our ordinary lives and trust to luck that the berries will stay on the tree? Be realistic!"

"I wish we could go back to the old ways," said Tortoise, "I don't see how we have come to be in such an awful muddle."

"It's not a muddle," said the deer solemnly. "It's a war."

Tortoise shivered: some sort of ugliness had seeped into their lives; it grew amongst them like a patch of poisonous toadstools pushing up through sweet grass. "Perhaps there is a solution," he said at last. "There are only a few days until the fruit is fully ripe: if neither side can trust the other side to be left alone to guard it, then maybe we should all guard the tree together."

"That's stupid," said the rabbits.

"Yes, it is," Tortoise agreed, "but it's better than having a war."

So that night all the animals settled down under the Rizzleberry tree to keep guard as one big group. They were all determined to stay wideawake but it wasn't long before their eyelids began to droop. They lay so close together around the trunk of their precious tree that not one of them could have made a move to steal the fruit without waking someone else. Tortoise did wake once in the night and thought he heard a noise like pebbles sliding down the rock. But he soon drifted off to sleep again.

In the morning, the animals woke up and yawned and stretched and looked up at the Rizzleberry tree to make sure everything was all right.

"Somebody has been stealing berries!" sang the finches furiously.

"Nonsense," said Tortoise, with a feeling of dread, "it looks all right to me."

But sure enough, near the top, a few branches stood out completely bare of fruit.

"It must have been the bats," snorted Pig.

"One of those monkeys climbed the tree in the dark," said the deer.

"I expect it was the finches themselves," said Lizard, "they just pretended to be surprised and cross when we woke up."

"Perhaps Tortoise has got a longer neck than we thought," said Mole.

"Nobody would have felt Grass Snake slithering between us while we slept," clucked the partridges.

"Maybe Bear came back specially to steal the berries," said Rabbit.

So there *was* a war at the foot of the Rizzleberry tree after all: but at least it was a war of words. Everyone accused everyone else, and nobody admitted anything. Tortoise looked for claw marks on the tree trunk or tufts of hair caught in the bark but there were no clues. "The thief must be invisible," he decided, "and weightless too – if he can walk all over us while we sleep and not wake us up."

That afternoon, Tortoise went to see his friends the fireflies to ask them a small favour. It was almost dark by the time he arrived back to take his place under the tree. He had made up his mind to stay awake right the way through until morning.

Tortoise felt tired and sad. The night stretched ahead of him, black and endless. Sometimes he would begin to slip into sleep and then wake with a sudden jolt: as if he had slid off the edge of the goats' track that led to Bear's cave. It was a hot and sticky night and Tortoise longed to be down by the cool sea. He could hear the leaves of the Rizzleberry tree trembling in the breeze . . .

What breeze! There was no wind – and yet the leaves were trembling. Tortoise was wide awake now. Something was happening in the tree.

"Wake up everybody!" shouted Tortoise. "Wake up!"

His friends the fireflies hovered above the tree in a great cloud; they gave out only a dim light, but enough for the animals to see who was in the tree.

There, with their hindlegs on the cliff face and their front legs making a bridge into the branches, were two goats.

They sprang back from the tree in alarm and clattered up the steep rock face and away.

The goats had never even thought of stealing from the Rizzleberry tree until Pig first planted the idea in their heads by asking them to be guards in his army.

"We must forgive the goats," said Tortoise when morning came and the indignant growls and snorts and twittering had died down.

But nobody could ever get close enough to the goats to tell them they were forgiven. They would just climb higher and higher up the mountainside, stopping to look back now and again, their defiant, distant eyes seeming to say: well, what *is* there to forgive anyway?

"Even today I still feel a bit sorry for the goats," sighed Tortoise when he had finished the story of the Rizzleberry War. "It must be a lonely life on top of the mountain."

"If they ever did come down," asked the young deer, "do you think they would steal from the Rizzleberry tree again?"

"I think they probably would," nodded Tortoise.

"In that case we must keep a guard on duty underneath the tree, night and day," said Pig, very seriously.

"No," said Tortoise with a smile, "I don't think that would be a very good idea."

The other animals laughed at Pig's foolishness. And in the end, so did Pig.

VIII
TURTLE'S MEDICINE

Tortoise settled down to sleep but he couldn't stop think-ing about the goats. Like Eagle in his empty sky and the coloured fish in their deep lagoon, the goats inhabited a separate, lonely world. Since the Rizzleberry War there had only been one occasion when the goats had touched the lives of the other animals.

"Tell us about it, Tortoise," begged the young deer, "please, tell us."

So though it was late and the first stars already winked in the dark roof of the sky, Tortoise told them.

The goats were very agile and sure-footed on steep rock but they did sometimes have accidents. One day a young and inexperienced goat was tiptoeing along a narrow path when the loose rock under his hooves suddenly collapsed and down he slid in a tumble of dust and pebbles. He would certainly have been killed had he not landed on a ledge only a little way below. On the ledge lay a large circle of dry twigs and leaves. It was an eagle's nest. The goat's fall was cushioned by the nest; he didn't even notice the bundle of squawking feathers he had sent spinning over the edge and into the tree tops far below. The goat scrambled back onto the path above, a little bruised, to look for his friends.

The eagle returned later and found her nest empty. What had happened? Where had her baby gone? She was in a panic. The eagle dived to where the cliffs met the tree tops; but the branches spread out so thick and so close against the rock face that, with her broad wings, she could not find a way through to the forest floor below. Her shadow put fear into the other birds nesting there and their calls of alarm drowned the squeaks of the baby eagle.

A little monkey happened to be exploring that part of the forest and he found the eagle chick crying in the undergrowth.

"Where do you come from, little fellow?" said the monkey, and the eagle chick told Monkey how he had been knocked out of his nest by a falling goat. "Never mind," said Monkey, "I'll put you back in your nest," and tucking the eaglet under one arm he went to the foot of the cliffs and began to climb.

Climbing was what this monkey loved best: rocks or tree trunks, it didn't really matter which. He had already climbed all the tallest trees in the forest – except the Snake Tree – and he had been wandering around that day just in case there was a really special challenge he might have overlooked.

It wasn't long before Monkey was high above the trees and putting the baby eagle back into its rather flattened nest.

"Goodbye then," he said cheerfully. He was just lowering himself back over the ledge when something hit him so hard it knocked all the breath out of him; letting go with his arms and legs, he rolled down the cliff and into the trees below. The eagle had asked no questions; she had seen Monkey with his hand in the nest and had decided he was to blame.

Monkey lay where he had fallen and was glad to be alive. But his tail hurt terribly and his legs felt very strange. "That's all the thanks I get for helping out," he cried, and pulling himself up he headed painfully for home.

The further he went, the more his tail hurt and the more tingly his legs felt. By the time he reached his home tree on the edge of the forest he felt very strange indeed. His mother was furious with him: "You are very foolish to have gone anywhere near Eagle's nest," she said, "we've always told you to keep well away from the eagles." Monkey felt too ill to argue.

Then his mother comforted him and gave him a big monkey-hug.

"I'm only cross because I'm worried," she said. "The best cure for you is a good night's sleep."

And Monkey did sleep, but his dreams were full of huge shadowy wings and cruel curved beaks that pecked at his tail. And in the morning when he woke, Monkey couldn't feel his legs at all.

"Don't be unhappy," said his mother when he burst into tears, "I'm sure you'll be all right soon, you are probably just a bit stiff and bruised." She brought him some juicy fruit to eat and made him a comfortable bed of leaves on the forest floor. As the days went by, Monkey did begin to feel a bit better: except in his legs – he still couldn't move them or even feel that they were there.

His friends came to see him and tried to cheer him up.

"Don't worry," they said. "You'll soon be the monkey you used to be. Just give your legs a chance to recover."

But Monkey was miserable; how would he ever climb again without the use of his legs?

"Things will improve, I'm sure they will," said Pig confidently.

"You will get better," clucked the partridges, "you wait and see."

"Everything takes time to heal," said his special friend, Coati, "be patient and hopeful."

But Monkey lay on his bed of leaves and watched the others sliding down the waterfalls and swinging in the trees and he was filled not with any hope, but with envy.

The other monkeys saw his longing and made an effort to include him in their games. They carried him through the branches and swung him by his arms, but never very high or very fast because it would have been dangerous. Monkey was glad to be up amongst the leaves again and to feel the wind in his ears but somehow it wasn't at all the same.

"The trouble is," he said to Coati, "they are very kind, but all the time I know that they are aching to leave me and get back to their own games. And who can blame them? I am just a burden to everybody."

"Nonsense," said Coati, "nothing has changed, you are still our good friend."

Every day, after his games, Monkey asked to be carried down to a shady spot on the edge of the beach. Then he would tell his friends to leave him. He would sit under the trees staring out to sea, watching the waves rolling in over the reef.

Coati was worried by Monkey's sad sea-watching, and he made up his mind to go and find some medicine for Monkey's useless legs.

"Ask Pig," suggested Monkey's mother, "he knows all about strange roots and fungi."

But Pig laughed and said he only knew which plants made him sick.

"Ask Badger," Pig said, "he's always saying how he knows everything."

But although Badger knew which leaves to rub on a nose stung by bees, he had heard of no plant to mend a broken monkey.

The squirrels had a store of berries that put fire in your tummy and helped you to sleep when it was very cold, but nothing that might bring back life to tingly legs.

Even the deer knew of no herb or flower which might cure Monkey's legs. "You could ask Turtle, I suppose," they said. "This is the season to find her. She comes to the beach at the end of the island where the sun rises, and there she lays her eggs."

Coati thanked the deer and set off at once to find Turtle. He travelled through the night, following the fringe of sea as it washed in and out over the moonlit sand. By morning he'd reached the far end of the huge curving beach and there he found the female turtle digging a hole for her eggs.

"The deer say that you are very wise," said Coati, "and coming from the sea you know things that we can never know." And then Coati told Turtle about Monkey's accident and how even though Monkey's friends now did everything for him, he was still miserable and sat watching the waves and wishing he was dead.

"We keep telling him he'll wake up one morning and everything will be fine again," said Coati, "but he's just empty of hope."

"Did you say you want him to walk again," said Turtle carefully, "or to get better?"

Coati was surprised, "Aren't they one and the same thing?"

"Not necessarily," said Turtle.

Coati didn't understand.

"Do you really want Monkey to get better?" asked Turtle.

"Of course I do," replied Coati.

"Will you do exactly what I say?" said Turtle.

Coati nodded. "I think so."

Turtle now looked Coati in the eyes with a strange ocean-deep stare. "You must tell Monkey that he will never get better; that there is no medicine for his useless legs, and that he will never again be the monkey he was."

Coati was horrified. "Do you call that good advice?" he cried. "I call it a death sentence. You are nothing but a mean ugly old sea monster!"

But the turtle ignored him and returned to her digging.

"What a wasted journey," muttered Coati to himself as he headed back along the beach. He was very tired and the noise of the waves booming on the sand made it difficult for him to think. All the way home, Coati tried to work out *why* Turtle had behaved in such a heartless way.

Towards the end of day he drew near the beach where Monkey usually sat on his own in the shade. But today Monkey was not alone. A whole crowd of excited animals was with him, waiting for Coati's return.

"What have you brought Monkey?" they called out.

"What did Turtle say?"

"Where's the medicine then?"

Coati looked at their hopeful faces, he felt ashamed to have come back empty-handed.

"Turtle has this advice for Monkey," he said at last. A hush came over the animals. "Monkey will never walk or climb like he used to. There is no cure or medicine for his useless legs, and they will never get any better."

The animals drew in their breath; they were shocked, and embarrassed too, because Coati had said out loud what each of them had secretly been thinking for quite some while. They muttered excuses and drifted away into the forest to get on with their lives.

Only Coati remained.

Monkey was astonished. Turtle's cure wasn't at all what he'd expected. He stared out to sea and had a long think.

"Who cares," he said at last, shrugging his shoulders, "I'd climbed every tree on the island anyway."

He turned to his friend. "Thank you, Coati," he said, "I needed to be told the truth, otherwise I would have been sitting around until the end of my life just waiting for my legs to get better."

Monkey suddenly felt more hopeful: maybe there were still exciting things to do in life. Perhaps I could try and climb the easiest trees again, he thought, using just my arms and tail.

By the time he and Coati had found the other animals, Monkey was full of new ideas. "I'll need your help to begin with," he said, "but after that I won't want any special treatment."

Every day Monkey did exercises to make his arms and tail stronger. He practised by holding on to a loop of creeper and pulling himself up and letting himself down many times in a row. He balanced heavy stones in his hands and pushed them up and down above his head until his shoulders ached. Soon he had bigger and better muscles than any of the other monkeys.

Coati organised the building of a sleeping platform high in the branches of a twisted starleaf tree. The platform had a fence around the sides to stop Monkey rolling over the edge in his sleep and a lovely woven roof to keep him dry. Hanging from the edge of the platform and reaching to the ground was a ladder made from strong sticks and twisted ivy. Tied to a branch above the roof were many lengths of creeper; these had been stretched and tied to other trees in the clearing so that it was easy for Monkey to travel from tree to tree.

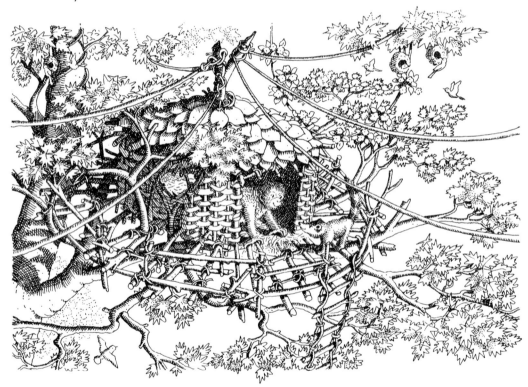

"It's fantastic," said Monkey when Coati showed him over his new home, "thank you all for making it."

Monkey was much more cheerful now. It wasn't long before he had climbed some of the easier trees in the forest without the help of any ladders or ropes. It didn't matter that he had climbed them before as a baby monkey.

"What an adventure," said his friend, Coati, "to start a new and different life."

"Yes," said Monkey. "If it hadn't been for Turtle's medicine, I'd still be staring out to sea."

Tortoise had come to the end of his story.

"Did anyone ever thank the turtle?" asked one of the young deer.

"I don't think she expected any thanks," said Tortoise, "she knew how hard it would be for Coati to follow her advice."

"I would love to see a turtle," said the young deer.

"Turtle is only here for a very short time," said Tortoise. "Her young hatch in the sand and then they too slip into the sea and are gone. Her underwater world is a very different place to ours."

Tortoise left the animals then and went down to the very edge of the lagoon. Sometimes he was able to see right into the beautiful clear rockpools, with their gardens of coloured weeds and rainbow shells. But it was night now and the surface of the water was dark and wind-ruffled and hid everything beneath it.

How strange it must be, thought Tortoise looking out to sea, to have no edge to one's world. We have a beach; we know the shape of our island and just how far we can go. But Turtle can swim away in any direction and keep going – her world has no limits, no ending. She can, if she chooses, swim on for ever and ever and ever.

IX
THE SNAKE TREE

"Why are we not allowed to climb the Snake Tree?" asked one of the little monkeys when Tortoise had settled down for an evening of stories and memories. "It looks such an easy tree to climb," the monkey went on, "it's the biggest and tallest tree on the whole island; it would be such fun to reach the top."

Tortoise put on his most serious face. "You know very well it is absolutely, completely, and utterly forbidden to even think of climbing the Snake Tree; to even touch its lowest branches."

"But why?" the little monkey persisted.

Tortoise was just about to get very cross when he realised that the monkey needed something more than a rule and a threat – he was old enough for an explanation.

"Settle down around me then," said Tortoise with a sigh, "and I will tell you the story of Porcupine. It's a frightening story and when I've finished you won't have any more questions about the Snake Tree."

Porcupines are good climbers. By day they sleep in caves or hollows, but at night they climb trees and eat bark, which they find nourishing and delicious. When Porcupine was young he loved climbing; it was the only thing he was any good at. He had many noisy young friends: tiny mischievous monkeys; boisterous badgers; naughty little wild pigs. They were always in trouble, daring each other to do sillier and yet sillier things. The piglets came home again and again with scratched and bleeding snouts; the monkeys suffered bruised bottoms and sprained tails; the badgers ended up stung all over by angry bees. But Porcupine was usually lucky – until the day his friends dared him to climb to the top of the Snake Tree.

Porcupine had an awful cold sick feeling when his friends first suggested it. Everybody knew how important it was to keep well away from the Snake Tree. But the more he thought about it, the less terrible the idea became. If there was anything really bad about it, thought Porcupine, then surely somebody would have told us exactly what the danger was. It's probably just because we'll get dirty, or too tired, or because there's something really delicious at the top. The adult animals were like that: rules often seemed to be for their own convenience or simply to be obeyed because they themselves had obeyed the same rule when they were young.

My mother is Porcupine the famous conjuror, he thought, but I will be known as Porcupine 'the nothing', unless I do something special in my life. The idea of climbing to the top of the Snake Tree, the highest and only unconquered tree on the island, became more and more attractive to him.

One night, when he and his mother were moving from tree to tree, chewing bark, Porcupine slipped away. I'll just have a look at the Snake Tree, he thought, to see how difficult a task it's going to be.

The undergrowth became thinner and thinner as Porcupine neared the clearing where the Snake Tree stood: it was as if the grass and weeds had grown sick. Soon there was only dry earth beneath his paws. The moon threw a criss-cross of shadows over the forest floor. Porcupine could hear no rasping or clicking of insects, no gurgling streams, no comforting song from the night finches.

The clearing was still and dead.

There stood the tree. The base of its trunk was enormous, as solid and dark as rock. The lower branches were themselves as thick as tree trunks, they spread out sideways in every direction before bending upwards and disappearing into the canopy of leaves above.

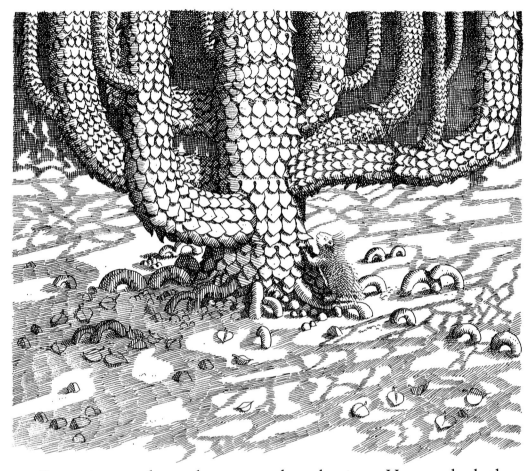

Porcupine trod gently across the clearing. He touched the bark. From a distance he had thought it was smooth, but in fact it was covered in large scales like a snake's skin. The scales pointed downwards. Every now and again there was a ring of loose scales which stuck out slightly. If you put your paw up underneath these loose scales, there you found a useful ridge to hold onto. It would be as easy to climb the Snake Tree as climbing Monkey's stick and ivy ladder.

Porcupine felt a fluttering in his chest as if he had breathed in a large dragonfly. The bark of the Snake Tree gave out a lovely perfume, an exciting smell that made Porcupine feel eager to begin; a smell that made him feel everything would be all right and that at the top there would be something especially nice waiting for him.

I will just go a little way up tonight, he thought, to see what it's like.

He chose one of the side branches that almost brushed the ground before it turned skywards. He pushed one paw under a loose ring of scales and there his claws found a ridge to hook onto. His other paw he slipped under the next loose row of scales slightly higher up and there he found another ridge – see, it was easy!

In no time at all he had pulled himself to a giddy height above the clearing. I will carry on until I reach a good turning-around point, he thought. And he climbed a bit higher. Soon I will reach a good place to rest, he thought. And he climbed a bit higher. I will wait until I get a chance to cross over to another tree, he thought, and then I'll be able to get down. And he climbed a bit higher still.

Porcupine soon realised that there were no good turning-around points; no convenient places to rest; and no chance of crossing to another tree. A sick, cheated feeling began to spread to his arms and legs. He was suddenly very afraid.

Climbing upwards, it was simple to see which rows of scales were loose and hid the easy hand-holds; but looking downwards the scales appeared to be all the same. Like snakeskin – which is rough to the touch if you stroke it one way, yet streamlined and smooth when you stroke it the other – the bark of this tree made it easy to go up and impossibly slippery to go down. And worse still, though it was dry when Porcupine climbed up, the pressure of his feet and body on the bark produced a thin oily juice which ran out from under each scale and down the branches of the tree.

Porcupine kept climbing. He knew now that the tree had tricked him. It no longer had an exciting perfume – it smelled of rotting fish and toadstools. He shouted out for his mother, but the spiked leaves of the Snake Tree muffled his cries.

"I am too tired," he said, "I shall fall, I know I will."

But there was no stopping now, the trunk and its thick branches pointed on and upwards. Hearing the wind rattling the leaves and seeing flecks of moonlight on the branches, Porcupine knew he had already climbed clear of all the other trees in the forest.

"I am Porcupine, the first climber of the Snake Tree," he

whispered to himself, "and I am surely going to die because of it."

It wasn't long before Porcupine reached the very top of the tree. On the tip of each branch grew a huge flower. The fleshy petals of each flower formed a cup big enough to have held even Pig. Porcupine pulled himself up between the rubbery petals and lay panting inside the flower.

The sky over Turtle beach was already turning pink. The sun would soon be up. Porcupine was too frightened to appreciate the view he had of the island. In the centre of the flower, rainwater had gathered. It lay there forming a pool and the slippery petals of the flower led down to the sweet-smelling water. Porcupine was thirsty. Digging his claws into the petals he crouched and touched the water with just the tip of his nose: "Ouch!" A terrible pain like a wasp sting burned on the part of his nose that had touched the liquid. Porcupine jerked back – it wasn't just his sore nose that worried him. Under the surface of the stinging juice he could see a brown sludge of drowned flies and moths and there, in the very deepest part of the flower pool, a scattering of little white bones. So, he was not the first creature to reach the top of the Snake Tree. Porcupine now understood how the tree trapped and digested its food. It had led him here and now it waited. Porcupine wouldn't be able to stay awake for ever. Eventually he would fall asleep and roll down the smooth petals into the pool at the heart of the flower.

Porcupine's mother was very worried. She had spent all night searching for her youngster, calling for him through the forest.

"I know the mud in the frog's swamp has sucked him under," she cried to the deer, "or else he has gone to the beach to play and been pulled out to sea by a freak wave."

But nobody had seen young Porcupine near the swamp or down by the sea, so his mother kept imagining other and more awful things that might have happened to him. The finches said they would fly up and down the island and see if they could spot Porcupine: perhaps he had fallen from a tree and banged his head, or got his foot tangled up in a creeper. The finches searched beneath and above every tree on the island, except the Snake Tree – they avoided it. The tree was always empty of birds. It was a bad place. Porcupine would not be there.

But Porcupine *was* there. He poked his head out between the petals of the hideous flower that had captured him and cried for his mother. Far below lay the forest, the tree tops bunched like cushions of moss on a boulder. Flocks of searching finches skimmed over the trees like shoals of tiny fish and he could see the lines of white waves curling onto the shore, but too slow and silent they moved, like in a bad dream.

At last the pelicans joined the search, flying higher and more steadily than the finches. They checked the steep cliffs of Firefly Mountain and the isolated rocks far out on the reef. And last of all they flew low over the top of the Snake Tree. There was Porcupine.

"We'll never get him down," said Pig, when the pelicans reported back to him. "Nobody else is going to climb the tree and no bird can land up there safely."

"And even if we did," said the pelicans, "we couldn't fly Porcupine out of the flower. He's too prickly to touch and he weighs as much as a fat rabbit."

"We could ask Beaver to chop the tree down," said Pig. But the pelicans shook their heads, it seemed there was no sensible solution. "We'll go and ask Monkey if he has an idea," said the pelicans, "but we won't tell anyone else: Porcupine's mother would be just *too* upset if she knew what had happened."

Monkey was in his house high in the starleaf tree. "In the old days I might have climbed the Snake Tree with a length of creeper and rescued him myself," said Monkey; but he couldn't think of a plan.

When the pelicans flew back to Pig, Monkey sat looking at the humming-birds hovering over the forest flowers and at the weaver finches busy building their basket nests. And as he sat, an idea blossomed in Monkey's mind in the same way as tightly furled petals in a bud open out into a big and colourful flower. But the idea frightened Monkey too; and a coldness, like the shadow of an eagle's wings, came over him.

To begin with, Monkey asked the weaver finches to weave him one of their basket nests, but a much bigger basket than usual, big enough to hold a piglet or a baby monkey. "It must be very light and very strong," said Monkey. He told the finches to build the basket right on top of the starleaf tree.

While the weaver finches were busy, Monkey set out for Firefly Mountain, swinging by his arms from the spider's web of creepers that the other monkeys had built for him. He was very afraid of what he had to do, but at the same time he was filled with a terrible determination to do it. "You fool, you idiot," he kept muttering, "turn back, let someone else think of a way to rescue Porcupine."

Soon the net of overhead creepers came to an end and Monkey was forced to swing to the ground and make his way through the undergrowth as best he could. It was easier when he got to the foot of the mountain; Monkey's arms were strong and his hands clever at finding cracks and ledges. It wasn't long before the last branches had brushed against his back and he was out on the bare cliff face.

"What are you doing here," cried Eagle when Monkey reached her nesting ledge, "you, of all the animals!"

"I came to ask you a favour," said Monkey. "I helped you once – though you never even knew it – and now you are the only one who can help me."

"You helped me?" said Eagle with a mocking laugh. "You came to steal my baby!"

"No, I found your chick at the bottom of the cliff," said

Monkey indignantly, "it was the goats who knocked him out of the nest. I was putting him back when you attacked me."

The eagle was silent. The mountain wind ruffled her golden feathers. She cocked her head and stared at Monkey with first one orange eye and then the other. Was this the truth or was it a lie? the piercing eyes asked. Eagle decided that Monkey was telling the truth: but she didn't apologise for the injury she had caused him. She only asked where she could find the starleaf tree and the weaver finches' basket. Then she spread her wings and flew from the ledge, leaving Monkey alone in the sun.

Eagle found the Starleaf tree, and the basket waiting in its topmost branches. She gripped the basket in her black talons and flew off towards the Snake Tree, its horrible purple flowers easily visible way above the tops of the other trees.

When she got there, the down-draught of Eagle's wing beats rattled the flower petals together. She hovered above each one like a giant searching bumblebee, and then she found Porcupine. With perfect control, Eagle lowered her yellow legs down into Porcupine's flower until the basket swung just above the surface of the stinging juice. "Climb in!" Eagle ordered Porcupine. And

Porcupine did as he was told. The basket was made of dry grasses and reeds that had been perfectly woven together. The finches had left a large round hole in the side as a doorway, and through this hole Porcupine scrambled.

At once, Eagle's powerful flapping quickened and she lifted the basket up and sideways, out of the flower and away. As Eagle flew higher and higher over the forest the wind whistled through all the tiny gaps in the woven walls of the basket. Porcupine put his head out of the round doorway and looked down on the whole of Firefly Island as no four-footed creature had ever done before. "I am Porcupine the Flyer," he sang in delight, "higher even than the Snake Tree. The first and last and only flying Porcupine!"

Porcupine knew that he could see everything now: there was the tiny drinking pool and the beach where they sat for their stories. There was Firefly Mountain, small as a pointed boulder, and, on the other side of it, the dark shaded woods that not even Tortoise had seen. Bear must be down there somewhere, fishing in the powerful rivers; berry-picking on the frosted mountainside. And the sea! How far and blue it reached on every side, curving away beneath the sky so that Porcupine could not see where, or even how, it ended.

Eagle folded her wings then and dropped like a boulder. The rushing air screamed and tore at Porcupine's basket. "Stop fooling about," cried Porcupine, "I shall be sick." The waves and the beach and the tree tops flew upwards to meet him. At the last moment, Eagle opened her wings and glided low and level just above the soft sand. She let go of the basket and flew off at once towards her mountain.

Porcupine climbed giddily out onto the hot sand. Eagle had gone without waiting for any thanks. And when the next wave came in and picked up the basket and carried it out to sea and sank it, Porcupine began to wonder whether any of it had ever really happened. His friends didn't believe his story and he could prove nothing. He never found out who had arranged his rescue. Pig, the pelicans and Monkey told no one what had happened: they wanted no special praise or thanks. It was enough for them to see young Porcupine grow up strong and prickly instead of being a little underwater pile of bones in a flower at the top of the Snake Tree.

"And that," said Tortoise, "is the end of Porcupine's story." Porcupine never became known as Porcupine the High Flyer or Porcupine the Great Climber: he just became Porcupine the Teller of Tall Tales – and he was happy enough to leave it at that. But his story was just frightening enough to keep any other youngster from ever daring to try and climb the Snake Tree."

"Why doesn't Beaver chop it down?" the little monkey asked Tortoise. "Then the last bad thing on Firefly Island would be gone."

"Beaver says the bark tastes of dead crabs," said Tortoise. "He can't bring himself to take even one decent bite out of it."

Tortoise looked at the animals around him. "We all want to be happy," he said. "Badness seems to sprout up here and there in our lives, and I don't understand why. Sore throats, broken legs, filthy tempers – we can't escape these things; we have to carry on regardless and live our lives around the edge of them. In the same way we must simply avoid the Snake Tree. Just because it grows here we mustn't let it spoil our enjoyment of the rest of our beautiful island home."

X
THE DAY OF THE
SHORTEST SHADOWS

Every hot season, when the midday shadow cast by Eagle Rock lay at its shortest, Tortoise would announce that the following day they would have their feast. Everyone looked forward to the feast; there was always good food and lots of games and, on the second day, a great race.

The monkeys prepared the food. It was something they had always done for the other animals since the beginning of memory, and they did it well. The fruit in the forest was now at its ripest, the flowers and leaves at their fullest.

The monkeys worked hard and spread out the feast in a clearing at the far edge of the island. What colour, what noise, when, towards evening time, the feasting at last began! Tortoise was happy: didn't this party show how all the different animals of Firefly Island were really one – they were friends, they feared no-one. Suddenly Tortoise felt a great love for all of them, large or small, ugly or beautiful.

Porcupine's mother who was a conjuror had a magic log to show them. It was hollow. She rested the log on a small pile of stones she had built. The log is empty, see! But Grass-snake goes in one end and disappears!

The animals cheered.

See! The log is empty, but suddenly, here is Dormouse! Closing each end with a large leaf, Porcupine muttered the magic words and held up the log again: Dormouse has gone!

The feasting animals held their breath. Porcupine closed the ends of the log again, rested it on the pile of stones, lifted her eyes to the stars, mumbled a spell and . . . a mist of moths and fireflies billowed out from each end of the log and hung like a dancing cloud above Porcupine! It was beautiful, it *was* magic; the animals applauded. Porcupine's conjuring went on and on.

Then one of the monkeys stood up and began juggling. Porcupine's show was over. She went and hid her magic log in the bushes; she didn't want anyone to spot the secret trap-door Woodpecker had drilled for her in its floor. There had been a lot of comings and goings through that hole during Porcupine's display. When at last no-one was looking, Grass-snake and Dormouse were glad to slip out of the hidden hollow in Porcupine's table of piled-up stones. The moths and fireflies had made Dormouse sneeze.

The moon rose from the ocean, huge and round. It was time to play hide-and-seek. "Remember, don't go far," called the monkeys as the other animals and birds spread out into the surrounding forest. The monkeys stayed in the clearing and shut their eyes, chanting together:

"Hop or tip-toe
Away you go,
Are we looking?
The answer's NO.

Creep and crawl
Slither or slide,
Choose the cleverest
Place to hide.

Too late to climb,
Too late to run,
We've hidden our eyes
But here we come!"

The monkeys found Lizard straightaway; he was easy to find for he had hiccups. Lizard was very upset; usually his camouflage was so good he did well at this game. "If I can't even win hide-and-seek, what *can* I win?" Lizard went off to sulk, he hated the great race, there was never any Rizzleberry fruit left by the time he reached the finishing line. "I'm just an ugly old fool," he muttered.

"Don't be unhappy, Lizard," said the monkeys, "you'll spoil everything."

Dormouse was the next to be found: she was still sneezing, so the monkeys knew exactly where she was. "Bother!" said Dormouse.

"Ouch!" cried one of the monkeys, who had brushed against Porcupine hiding under a thick bush. "If you'd kept your quills down, I would never have found you," he said.

The deer stretched their necks upwards and tried to look as much like tree trunks as possible. Pig lay on his back and pretended to be a rotten log. Tortoise was not difficult to find, even though Lizard was resting on his back – thinking Tortoise's bony shell was a large warm stone. The monkeys were not so easily fooled.

Nobody ever found Mole; every time he cheated and dug deep underground.

Grass-snake was the winner: he had wrapped himself around a tree like a length of creeper.

Everyone was tired out. "It's time to rest," said Tortoise, "but don't forget tomorrow is the day of the great race. Since it's impossible for anything as slow and ponderous as a tortoise to win, I shall travel overnight to the finish by the drinking pool. There I will wait and judge who is first across the line."

"When do we start?" chattered the chipmunks.

"As soon as the rising sun strikes the top of Firefly Mountain," replied Tortoise, "and remember, first one to the pool gets first picking from the Rizzleberry tree."

And leaving the rest of the animals, he set off into the dark forest so as to cross the island and be ready at the finishing line by morning. Tortoise wasn't aware he had a passenger, and Lizard lay so deeply asleep in the coolness of the night that he didn't realise he was getting a free ride. It was only when Tortoise had nearly reached the drinking pool that Lizard slipped off his back into a patch of deliciously soft grass; so smoothly did he slide from Tortoise's shell that he didn't even wake up.

Tortoise positioned himself at the finishing line and then he too fell asleep.

As soon as the far horizon began to brighten, the animals woke one by one and stretched and yawned and rolled in the dew. They lined up in the clearing where the feast had been held. They waited in silence, watching the peak of Firefly Mountain for that first orange light of the rising sun which meant the race should begin.

"There it is!" screeched the finches. At once the animals set off on their chosen routes into the forest.

"I'm as slow as Lizard," grumbled Porcupine as he waddled off into the trees, "I really don't know why I bother."

"It'll take all day," complained the rabbits, who might easily have won if only they didn't stop to nibble grass in the clearings.

The squirrels set off towards the mountain; they had a special plan all their own.

Dormouse had decided to cheat. "Otherwise I haven't got a chance," she reassured herself. A friendly pelican had agreed to help her, and not to tell anyone either. "Whatever you do, just keep your mouth shut," said Dormouse.

The frogs did quite well to begin with, but their legs got awfully tired.

Pig knew exactly which of his usual forest trails he'd follow – but so did the monkeys. Just as he'd got up speed, something always seemed to stop him in his tracks. The monkeys had dug a pit and disguised it with branches and leaves. Quail and Pheasant were so light on their feet that they scuttled over the top, but when Pig arrived, he crashed down into the pit. "It isn't fair!" he snorted, knowing who was to blame.

The monkeys built a delicate floating bridge of twigs and large leaves across a muddy pool. Pig thought it was a path and kept going. "What a fool I am!" spluttered Pig when he splashed hoof over snout into the ooze. There was a lot of laughter from the tree tops. The monkeys could well have been the first to reach Tortoise, but they were more interested in the outcome of their tricks than in winning anything.

Mole was deep in the earth and moving in the right direction, but he'd gone only a few feet when underground boulders put an end to his race.

The deer would easily have won, but as usual they kept stopping and flapping their ears and twitching their noses and sniffing the air, so they were always being overtaken.

Hedgehog was rather slow, except when going downhill: then he curled up in a ball and rolled.

As for Grass-snake, he usually went so smoothly and quietly that nobody ever knew where he was. But the monkeys had stopped him from going anywhere at all this time: they'd tied his tail in a knot around a tree root while he slept.

After a steep climb the squirrels reached the stream that cascaded all the way down Firefly Mountain to the drinking pool at the far end of the island. There they had hidden something rather special: a hollowed-out canoe that Woodpecker had helped them to build. "The second half of the race is going to be easy for us," they said with a laugh. But it wasn't quite as easy as they'd hoped!

Each animal dreamed of the solitary Rizzleberry tree that grew over the drinking pool and of how heavy its branches would be with the delicious red fruit which ripened only at this season of the longest day. The winner of the race was allowed to take his fill first; and the others – in order of finishing – to eat what was left. If Pig won there would be nothing left for the others! There was no taste as good as the Rizzleberry fruit; just the thought of it made your paws weak and fluttery.

Tortoise could tell, by the ripple of excitement spreading through the forest, that the leaders of the race were near. In fact, what with one thing and another, they were all very close together: anybody could win.

"Put me down!" called Dormouse to the pelican as they came in to land.

The squirrels had got a soaking in the mountain stream, they were wet and miserable.

"Come on! Come on!" cried Tortoise and the finches, as the noise of the race grew nearer: "Come on, not far, not far, hurrah, hurrah, you're winning, you're winning!"

Lizard woke up under his tent of grass; he was not yet fully warmed by the morning sun and therefore not very alert. But he heard Tortoise's cheering and encouragement.

"Winning?" said Lizard to himself. "Winning? Do they mean me?" And at that he pushed himself out into the sunlight and scuttled jerkily towards Tortoise's enthusiastic shouts.

"Really winning?" he panted. It hadn't seemed so difficult after all.

At the same time a line of assorted animals broke through the undergrowth into the clearing. It really was a race to see who would reach Tortoise first. "Come on, come on!" yelled Tortoise. "You can do it, Lizard, you CAN do it!"

And he did. Lizard was there first. What a smile spread across his face: "Me, a winner?" said Lizard with disbelief. "Really? It was nothing, easy, a pleasure in fact."

He was as surprised at his victory as anyone else, though he couldn't quite remember how he'd done it – he wasn't out of breath, his legs didn't ache, it had been effortless. I am a true athlete, thought Lizard to himself.

Now for the prize! Lizard ate as much of the Rizzleberry fruit as he could. He stood on Tortoise's back to reach it. He'd often tried to imagine what it would be like, but it was better than any of the tastes he'd invented – red and fizzy, cool and fruity. It was a good crop and the tree was heavily laden. There was plenty left for the others when Lizard lay burping and tight-bellied in the shade.

"And now to cool off," said Tortoise, for it was a very hot day. They made their way down to the little beach where the stream ran out into the sea. Here in the dappled shade they rested. Some of the animals went down to the waves to play. Pig lay in the stream. The deer drank and flicked the flies away with their long ears. The wind trembled in the leaves and flowers above them.

Tortoise was happy, he wanted this day to last forever, and in a way he knew it would. Even when, finally, his scaly skin fed the roots of the trees; when the finches bathed and drank in his hollow upturned shell – this day, this happiness he felt, would not have gone; nothing could destroy it. It would still be there in the forest like breathed-out air, like mist hanging as brightly as a cloud of stars or fireflies in the dark.